FICTION Hart, Carolyn G.
HART
Skulduggery.

DATE			

SKULDUGGERY

SKULDUGGERY

Carolyn G. Hart

Five Star
Unity, Maine

Five Star First Edition Mystery Series.
Published in 2000 in conjunction with
Tekno Books & Ed Gorman.

First Edition, Second Printing

Cover design by Carol Pringle.

Set in 11 pt. Plantin by Al Chase.

Printed in the United States on permanent paper.

Library of Congress Cataloging-in-Publication Data

Hart, Carolyn G.
  Skulduggery / by Carolyn G. Hart.
    p.   cm.
  ISBN 0-7862-2672-2 (hc : alk. paper)
  1. Women anthropologists — Fiction. 2. Chinatown (San Francisco, Calif.) — Fiction. 3. San Francisco (Calif.) — Fiction. 4. Treasure-trove — Fiction. I. Title.
PS3558.A676 S58 2000
  813'.54—dc21   00-030845

SKULDUGGERY

ONE

He may have followed me right from the first, from the moment I left the office. Or he may have waited for me in the shadows of the huge old pines that bordered the museum parking lot.

I paid no attention to the dark shadows of the pines, didn't listen for footsteps behind me. I was absorbed in my own thoughts, trying to remember if I'd bought lemons the last time I shopped. The avocados were just right for guacamole, but, of course, I had to have a lemon. I wanted this to be an especially nice dinner.

I unlocked the car door, slipped behind the wheel. An especially nice dinner. What a revealing thought. As I backed out of my parking slot, turned toward the street, my sense of well-being eroded. Did I want to show Richard how well I cooked? Did I judge that was what really mattered to Richard, a well-cooked meal, a comfortable household?

The car picked up speed. How silly to probe and test and weigh a vagrant thought. There was certainly nothing abnormal about liking comfort.

But did I want to be comfortable?

It is so easy to slide into something. So difficult to get out.

I braked at the corner, waited for the light to change. The red of the stoplight was dim and soft, insubstantial in the fog, that wraithlike fog that can slip up and down San Francisco's hills in winter.

When the light changed, I accelerated rapidly, impatient with myself. I had started home, hurrying happy, looking forward to a pleasant evening.

Pleasant. What an unremarkable word.

Don't be spiteful, Ellen, I told myself sharply.

So I was involved in my own thoughts, driving automatically, paying no attention to the traffic behind me. We are all the centres of our own existence. I knew as I changed gears, stopped, started, turned, that a hungry child cried in Mexico City, an old woman died in Cartagena, lovers kissed in London, but none of it was real to me. I was caught up in my own world, my own life, busy, intent, heading down a predetermined path, not really interested in what was happening to others.

But, sometimes, the unexpected happens, snatching us out of our routine, flinging us into someone else's life. It can be enough to turn our world around.

I caught mostly green lights so it only took fifteen minutes or so to get home, to the steep streets of Russian Hill. I parked, turning the wheels into the kerb, and hurried up the fog slick sidewalk to my apartment house. It stands, narrow and haughty, midway up the Hill. It had been, of course, converted from an old private residence which resulted in some peculiar wiring and odd placement of closets but the bay windows that jutted out over the street and the shiny golden real oak floors more than compensated. It was several miles from the museum, but, in the six months I had lived there, I had found every drive a new experience. Sometimes the sky was the soft blue of faded denim and a tangy sea-wet breeze rustled the pepper and eucalyptus trees. Sometimes a cloying fog hid gabled roofs, clung to street lamps, softened every outline into an impressionist vision.

I liked San Francisco, liked her many faces, liked her better every day I stayed.

Was I going to stay always?

I was climbing the narrow steps to the front door. I slowed.

Always is a long time. Was I ready for always?

I unlocked the door, stepped inside. And I don't suppose I checked to be sure the door pulled shut behind me. I was grappling with a heavy word.

Always.

One flight of steps, two, then the third floor and my apartment to the right. I was happy here in San Francisco. I loved my job. Loved it and was damn lucky to have it because there are lots of anthropologists and not nearly enough jobs to go around.

I unlocked my door, stepped inside, turned on the light. Closing the door, I slipped off my coat, hung it on the tree, but made no move toward the kitchen.

I looked around my living room, saw it for that instant from a stranger's eyes, the truly lovely small Persian rug, silver and blue, in front of the fireplace; the bookcases lining two walls, full of good, bad, indifferent books, most of them culled from secondhand shops, all of them read, some read often; the fist-sized walrus so delicately carved from driftwood by Maki, a hunter at the sealing camp in Alaska where I had spent last summer, compiling data on blood group genes. Every time I saw the carving, it brought the summer back so vividly, the endless day, the whirring swarms of mosquitoes, vagrant dogs, laughing children.

My room, echoes of my life.

In my mind, I saw Richard's apartment. Neater than mine, the books tidily arranged, Andrew Wyeth prints, a Muslim prayer rug, a Tiffany glass lamp hanging over the Edwardian pool table.

Compatible rooms.

Slowly I slipped off my gloves, dropped them and my purse on the end table.

Well, what the hell did I want?

Richard and I shared the same interests, the same back-ground. We could build a future together. But was it alto-gether too much sameness?

I walked toward the narrow kitchen with its old-fashioned gas range and white wooden cabinets and deep porcelain sink. I didn't have time to think, not if I hoped to fix dinner, bathe and dress before Richard came.

The shrimp must be cleaned, the batter made. Then I would cook the rice for the broccoli, cheese and rice casse-role. It needed at least half-an-hour to bake, sometimes longer, depending upon the oven's mood. I would bathe and dress, make the guacamole the last thing.

Richard liked to eat promptly at seven-thirty.

I liked to eat when I was hungry. Even if it meant sardines and cream cheese at two in the morning. I opened the small refrigerator, lifted out the plastic bag of fresh shrimp, dumped them on the drainboard and began to peel off the shells and lift out the gritty intestine.

Richard was thoughtful and kind and, moreover, a very at-tractive man. I liked his mouth, liked the way he touched me, liked the intent look in his dark blue eyes when he reached out to pull me close.

Yes. But, even so, would the two of us together, pleasant, compatible, well-adjusted, would we ultimately be just a teeny bit . . . boring?

What did I think I wanted?

Scooping up the shrimp shells, I stuffed them into the plastic bag then twisted its neck into a knot (to keep the odour in) and dropped it in the garbage pail. Now I needed egg, milk, a dash of salt, crackers.

I wasn't a schoolgirl. I knew that romance was its own cre-ation. So what did I want?

Unbidden, I remembered Bill. The rolling pin stopped,

the stack of crackers half crumbled. So long ago. Warm Arkansas summers, swimming in the lake, drive-in movies, high school sweethearts. Rowdy, exuberant, dictatorial, unpredictable Bill. Dead at twenty in the ugliness of Vietnam.

I moved the rolling pin jerkily, scattering crumbs along the counter top. I was brushing them back onto the waxed paper when I heard a knock at the front door.

Startled, I glanced up at the electric kitchen clock. No, it couldn't be Richard. Not yet. It wasn't even six yet.

I rinsed my hands, dried them and hurried to open the door.

He was half-turned, looking over his shoulder. He jerked around to face me. Emotion is communicable without any words. It doesn't take ESP to know if someone is angry or grieved—or excited.

He spoke my name so quickly I almost couldn't understand it.

"Dr Christie?"

I hesitated. I wasn't in the telephone book. I hadn't lived here long enough yet. And I didn't know him.

"Dr Christie?" His voice was sharp now, edged with impatience.

He was younger than I, slightly built, very handsome with black eyes, straight thick black eyebrows, skin the colour of dark summer honey, broad high cheekbones, a low-bridged nose. A classic Chinese face.

And, somehow, vaguely familiar.

"Yes," I said finally, warily, "I'm Dr Christie. What do you want?"

He looked over his shoulder again, quickly, tensely.

I, too, looked beyond him, down the flight of stairs.

A door shut downstairs and he flinched. Turning back to me, he said urgently, "Can I talk to you? Please?"

11

I don't know what he saw in my face, uneasiness rejection, withdrawal.

"You'll be glad you did," he said unexpectedly.

Why in the world . . .

"You are the bone lady. Aren't you?"

I stepped back to let him come in. As I did, I knew I was gambling. San Francisco is beautiful, exciting, glamorous and, as all big cities, dangerous as hell if you don't use your head.

I could imagine Richard's expression. Fastidious distaste. Letting in a roughly-dressed stranger, he would be appalled.

He hadn't thought the bone lady story funny at all. I had. Perhaps I lack the proper dignity. But, I don't think that's it. I just can't take anybody too seriously, much less myself. So the story hadn't bothered me.

I closed the door behind my unscheduled visitor and nodded toward the couch. He sat down stiffly, both feet flat on the floor, his hands in his lap. With the thumb and fore-finger of his right hand, he rubbed nervously on his left wrist.

I remembered that gesture. This afternoon, late in the af-ternoon, I had led a tour through the Early Man section of the museum. It was the usual pick-me-up crowd; students, lonely old men, children on a field trip, a sprinkling of affluent tour-ists. On the edge of the group, a young Chinese in a black-and-red checked flannel shirt had watched and listened and constantly rubbed that wrist.

"Who are you?" I asked sharply.

He shook his head at that. "It doesn't matter." He stared at me for a long moment and I wondered what he looked for. He saw a woman in her mid-twenties, crisply curling black hair, Irish blue eyes and what my mother called an aristo-cratic nose. My father called it 'damn noticeable'.

"You are Dr Christie?" he asked insistently. "Dr Ellen Christie?"

I nodded impatiently.

"I read about you in the newspaper, Dr Christie. You know all about bones."

I shrugged. "No one knows all about anything."

"But you are the bone lady?"

The bone lady.

My co-workers had loved the story, but I didn't mind their laughter. The reporter was young and he meant well. In my view that excused a lot.

It was an interesting story. Human bones fascinate everyone. These particular bones turned up during excavations for a new sewer line off the Embarcadero near Pacific. The workmen were shovelling, the bulldozer idled because a gas line ran through the area. Suddenly, one of them yelled out, "Hey, you guys, look at this!"

Digging stopped. The police came. The medical examiner was notified. Finally, after the bones were excavated carefully from the compacted sand, the Medical Examiner's office called the museum. Our department chairman often aided the police by studying odd skeletons that turned up. But the call came just before the Thanksgiving holiday and Dr Fernandez was out of town. I was the other physical anthropologist on the staff and I was happy to help out.

I spent an interesting afternoon reconstructing the skeleton, studying the size of the long bones, the dentition of the teeth—and the gaping hole in the top rear of the cranium.

It was murder, all right. But the murderer had long since met Judgment. Long since. I estimated the age of the burial at about seventy-five years ago and found I'd shorted it when I talked to the police lieutenant. Several loose brass buttons, a brass belt buckle and four coins were found beneath the bones. The coins were an 1856 one-dollar U.S. gold piece, an 1859 silver half-dime and two bronze two-cent pieces dated 1865 and 1867, so the bones had likely laid there nearer a hundred years.

The lieutenant told me something about the history of that section of San Francisco. It was infamous in the 1860s and 1870s for the abduction of seamen who were rounded up, drugged and hauled out to ships where they awoke at sea to find themselves treated as slave labour and bound for Shanghai.

I told him something of this victim, that he was a Caucasian male about nineteen years old, that his skull was unusually thin, that he had been slightly built, weighing perhaps one hundred and twenty to thirty pounds and standing five inches over five feet, that he had as a child broken his left leg and must have walked with a noticeable limp, and, that shortly before his untimely death he had suffered an impacted wisdom tooth which must have been very painful.

"Goddam," the lieutenant laughed, "what colour eyes did he have?"

And that was all there was to it. An interesting experience but unimportant in the scheme of my life. When the telephone at my office rang the next day and it was a reporter, a friend of the lieutenant's, I thought the same.

Someone dropped a clipping of the reporter's story on my desk several days later. I had missed it in the paper. I will say that the reporter had an interesting style. The story began:

"San Francisco's bone lady divines the past, not with tarot cards or crystal balls, but with broken clumps of bone rudely shaken from a century-old grave. And finds nothing the least unusual in doing so.

Dr Ellen Christie, a physical anthropologist, responded to a call from the police department for help in identifying bones discovered Wednesday by a street crew excavating on the Embarcadero near Pacific.

As Dr Christie explains, 'It is possible to reconstruct . . .' "

Someone at the museum with a gleeful sense of humour snapped my picture and put the developed snapshot on the department bulletin board with a bone neatly sketched in my mouth.

It was the subject of a good deal of ribald comment for a while. But, all things pass, and, eventually, no one mentioned the story any more. Or called me bone lady.

Until tonight. Now this tense excited young man wanted to know, it was important for him to know, whether I was the bone lady.

TWO

"I'm Ellen Christie. I'm a physical anthropologist. I know something about bones."

"Old bones? Fossils?"

He had my attention. I pushed away from the door, came closer to the couch, looked down at his young anxious face.

"Yes," I said quickly. "As a matter of fact, I know quite a bit about fossils. Why?"

His head swivelled around, his eyes searching the shadows of the room.

"I live alone."

He nodded, then spoke so softly that I strained to hear. "I have a skull. I want to show it to you. I want to know if you recognize it."

"A skull. Where did it come from?"

He shook his head.

I shrugged. "You must understand," I began and I must have sounded professorial, "a skull out of context can be meaningless . . ."

I broke off for he was shaking his head again, sharply.

"Not these bones."

Bones, he said. Bones, plural. He wanted to show me a skull. But he had bones.

I felt suddenly breathless. I stared at his handsome face, at his smooth dark cheeks, and saw the thin film of sweat beading his mouth and the rigid line of his jaw.

Whatever he had, he was wild with excitement. And he would show the skull to me.

"Where are the bones?" I looked toward my door. "Are they here? Do you have them . . ."

"They're in a safe place. Not here. If you'll come with me . . ."

The telephone rang.

He jumped up, whirled toward the phone, then stopped, almost in a crouch, and looked at me.

"No," he said sharply as I moved toward my desk. Then, embarrassed, he spread his hands. "I'm sorry. But, please, don't say anything about me."

I nodded.

It was Richard.

"Oh. Oh yes, Richard, that's thoughtful of you, yes, a sauterne would be excellent. But, Richard, I'm sorry, we can't have dinner after all . . . oh no, everything's fine . . . it's an old friend, Sally Morris, you've heard me speak of her . . . no, at the airport of all things, en route to Honolulu, a layover . . . I know, I'm disappointed, too, but you know how these things are . . . I am sorry . . . yes, tomorrow night then."

As I put down the receiver, the young man smiled at me and the smile reached deep into his black eyes.

I moved quickly then, putting the shrimp in the refrigerator, pouring the cracker crumbs into a plastic bag, wiping clean the counter top. It was only as I slipped on my coat that I paused for an instant. I had offended Richard. But, dammit, if an old friend had come to town, he should have been more understanding.

I buttoned my coat.

It had been so easy to lie to Richard.

I was reaching out to open the door when the young man raised his hand.

"Wait a minute, Dr Christie. I wasn't going to say anything, but, I can't ask you to come . . . and just keep quiet.

17

People have been following me. This isn't safe, you know. I lost them, I'm almost sure. But, still, if you don't want to take a chance, I'll understand."

He stood so close I could smell pine-scented shaving lotion and the fog-dampened wool of his checkered shirt.

Whatever threat he perceived, he believed in it.

I hesitated.

Richard, I knew, would send this young man away, tell him to bring his bones, whatever they were, to the museum. Make an appointment. Richard had turned down an expedition to Africa. Too much unrest, he had said. Odd, I hadn't thought about that refusal in several months. I had hidden my surprise at that decision from Richard.

Surprise. And disappointment?

I looked at the handsome young man standing so near me. He waited tensely, hoping.

"Do you have a car?" I asked.

He smiled. "I have my motorcycle, Dr Christie. You can ride behind me. It isn't far."

It was the motorcycle that turned the balance. I was twenty-seven years old and I had never ridden on a motorcycle.

I always felt, later, that the ride was worth it. Plunging up and down fog-hung streets, the vibration of the motor, the sensation of speed and freedom, it was unlike anything I had ever done.

I had an idea of our destination when we swung off Hyde onto Pacific and I was sure of it when we turned south on Stockton.

I had been to Chinatown once before on a cold, damp day in August. To lunch in a delightful and delightfully inexpensive restaurant. When I ate that lunch, I had no idea why it was so good or why it was so cheap in comparison with other restaurants in San Francisco. I thought, if I thought at all, that here was an old-fashioned lure for tourists, buildings with their corners uptilted, Chinese characters in neon, shops with dried seaweed, ginseng and pressed ducks. Exotic, oriental, not quite real.

I didn't think of it as a place where people lived.

We passed closed and shuttered shops, laundries, groceries, then swung right down a narrow street. I was lost, of course. We were somewhere in Chinatown. Then the cycle slowed, turned into the darkness of a narrow alleyway. The noise of the engine was magnified against the looming brick walls. He stopped next to a wooden rack holding garbage pails. I climbed off and removed the helmet he had given me and watched as he locked the cycle and the helmets to the garbage rack.

He took my arm. "This way," and he led me deeper into the darkness. I looked back once. The fog already hid the pails and the cycle though the smell of rotting fish and cabbage and spoiled fruit followed us. The only light in the alleyway came from a distant street lamp, but he seemed to know his way. We had gone perhaps fifteen yards when his hand tightened on my arm and he stopped. I waited with him and heard too the soft slap of approaching footsteps.

He looked back the way we had come, hesitated, then pulled me along. We walked on and the footsteps came nearer. It was an old man, an old bent man in a heavy black wool suit, carrying a string bag, who came toward us. He raised his head and peered through the darkness and fog.

My companion ducked his head into his collar, turned a shoulder toward the old man and we passed without a word. I looked back over my shoulder and saw black eyes watching us sharply.

We hurried on, brick walls glistening on either side of us,

uneven brick underfoot, and I wondered where this alley led.

But we didn't leave the alley.

I wouldn't have seen the door, would have passed it by, but he nudged me to the right and there, set flush with the wall, was a red door, almost indistinguishable from the brick around it.

He dropped my arm, fumbled in his pocket and drew out keys hung on a circle of metal. The door opened slowly, creaking on its hinges, opened onto darkness.

"Step just inside," he whispered. "I'll leave the door a little ajar so we can see our way down the steps. I don't want to use a light yet."

We walked down steep wooden steps, down, down, down into darkness and the air was cold and stale, smelling of mould and dust and age.

Emptiness. You can feel emptiness. There was no one anywhere. I knew it and I wondered, for the first time, if I had made a mistake. A serious mistake. Every city has its abandoned, disintegrating, boarded-up hulks. Why would he bring me . . .

My foot jolted against the floor because the step I had expected was not there.

We stopped there at the foot of the stairs and I felt him listen. I listened, too, but there was nothing at all to hear, not the faintest sigh of a sound.

"It's empty," I said sharply.

He started at the sound of my voice.

"Be quiet," he whispered.

I was quiet, caught up in his intensity, listening, waiting.

Then I heard a little spurt of air, a sigh of relaxation and he spoke aloud though still quietly. "We're okay. It's supposed to be empty and it is."

A tiny pencil of light flickered on and he pointed it ahead. I saw rockhard earth and wondered where there was a building so old that its cellar was of dirt, not brick.

"This way." We moved slowly down a narrow hallway, skirting a row of boxes stacked against a brick wall, past wooden cupboards, the wood splintery and unfinished. We walked to the end of the hall to a closed door. He pulled the keyring out of his pocket again, tried several keys until he found the right one.

He flipped a wall switch and a single low-watt bulb dangling from the low ceiling, came on. It was a small rectangular room and I hesitated in the doorway for this was, unexpectedly, someone's home. A narrow camp bed sat against the opposite wall. Above it hung a bulletin board with every inch covered, snapshots, yellowed newspaper clippings, ticket stubs, menus, and, in the top right-hand corner, a faded khaki Army cap. A tool bench ran along the wall to the right. To the left were neatly stacked orange crates, holding flour and sugar canisters, a few canned goods, a stack of old iron pans, a shelf full of Chinese paperback books. A hot plate sat atop a metal drum.

A single wooden chair sat next to the tool bench. The young man pulled it out.

"Here, Dr Christie. You'll be safe here. I'll hurry."

He was at the door before I spoke.

"Wait, please. Where are you going?"

"To get the skull." He smiled, a quick almost impish smile. "It's in a safe place. No one would ever think . . . Anyway, I'll be right back."

I watched the door close then turned and walked to the chair and sat. But I no more than sat than I was on my feet again, pacing nervously up and down the narrow room. I had come to this quiet cold room, followed a stranger, because I had an inkling what those bones might be.

There are bones that would bring danger in their trail. Any anthropologist knows which bones. Bones that had surfaced briefly on the other side of the world then been swept away in the chaos of World War II. Bones that had been in the news of late years, whispers that they were in Macao, in New York, in Shanghai, in Melbourne, in the California hills.

One man had publicly offered one hundred and fifty thousand dollars for the bones.

Others might pay even more.

I paced up and down, up and down. Was it possible, was it remotely possible that . . .

I heard the door open and whirled around. He clutched a YMCA tote bag. I thought he was certainly right on one count. You wouldn't expect to find the contents of that bag in the average YMCA locker.

I was close beside him when he put the bag down in the centre of the work bench. Unzipping the bag, he reached inside and lifted out a powerful lantern-type of flashlight and sat it on its base. Now there was plenty of light, light enough to see the faintest of scratches on the surface of the workbench. He reached into the bag again, drawing out what looked to be a clump of soiled clothes, a thick grey cotton sweatshirt wadded into an uneven ball.

He unwound the sweatshirt and my breath caught in my chest. My god, it was, it really was!

I reached out, took the skull and held it gingerly, turning it slowly this way and that in the bright beam from the lamp.

You would never mistake it for a modern skull, but, all the same, it was man and not simian. The most noticeable single aspect of the skull was the spectacular projection of the brow, a horizontal bar of bone extending the full width of the lower margin of the forehead. Lightly, I touched that bar of bone. It was this that had given Peking Man his distinctive heavybrowed appearance.

There, I had thought it, put recognition into form. Peking Man. One of man's earliest ancestors, his fossil bones had been discovered in China 40-odd years ago.

Bones, irreplaceable, indescribably valuable, and given up for lost after their disappearance in 1941.

I traced the slight bulge of the forehead and the relatively flattened top of the skull. The side walls of the skull sloped inward and upward. I turned the deep yellow skull to look at the back and there was a bony ridge at its base, just above the nape of the neck. And, along the top of the cranium, a pronounced ridge extended lengthwise along the middle of the crown.

Oh yes, here in my hand I held a fossil that would rate inch-thick headlines all around the world, an almost complete skull of Peking Man—or a magnificent counterfeit.

I looked warily at the young man who was watching me so closely, intent upon my appraisal.

"Where . . ." I began.

He shook his head. Firmly.

"It's Peking Man, isn't it?" he asked.

My fingers touched again that bar of bone above the eye sockets. Five hundred thousand years ago, flesh covered these bones. The face had jutted forward with scarcely any chin, but, had we stood face to face, we would have recognized our kinship. Early man, but, man, nonetheless. Eyes had looked out of these sockets, eyes that watched anxiously when storm clouds towered above the valley, eyes that softened in love, closed in sleep, wept with loss and pain.

I looked into living eyes that watched me so intently.

I touched the cheekbones then slipped my hand again to the back of the skull and the strong bony ridge near its base. Yes, oh yes, I thought. But I began, "In a laboratory . . ."

He reached out, grabbed my arm. "Don't try to kid me," he said angrily.

I shrugged. "I can't tell you. It doesn't matter what I think . . . or guess. If you want proof, you'll have to submit the skull and the other bones for tests. Then you'll know."

"But you know now."

I pulled away and once again spread my fingers softly on the ancient yellow hard fossil. "Oh yes," I said softly, "I think you've turned the trick. I don't know where or how, but I think you've come up with the most famous lost bones in the world."

He expelled a breath gently, slowly, and the tension eased out of his face. He had not then been absolutely sure of his find.

My hand curved around the back of the skull. "I never dreamed, ever, that I would touch a fossil like this." What did it mean to him that we had, in this room, in our hands, a scientific treasure? "Do you know," I asked urgently, "do you have any idea how valuable this skull is?"

"Yeah, I think I do."

I didn't want to let go of the skull. I didn't want to do anything but hold it, touch it, look at it. But, I knew my responsibility.

"Look," I said abruptly, "we need to get the rest of the bones, get them all together, put them in a safe place. Let me call the chairman of my department at the museum. He will know best how to protect the fossils, who to get in touch with and . . ."

He was shaking his head.

I suppose all along I must have known. Still, I was shocked. My face must have shown that shock.

A dull flush moved under his honeydark skin but his eyes were implacable.

"Then why bring me here?" I asked angrily.

"I'm sorry, Dr Christie, sorry as hell. But, I wasn't sure. I thought it was Peking Man, but I couldn't be sure. I had to be absolutely sure before . . ."

He didn't finish. He didn't have to. I understood. He had to be certain of his ground before he looked for a buyer. But, still, I asked, "And now that you are sure?"

His eyes shifted away from me.

"Please," I said swiftly, "I'm sure there must be a reward of some sort . . ."

"Oh no, Dr Christie." He laughed and it wasn't a pleasant laugh. "Give the boy a nice pittance and thank him." He shook his head again. "No. If I handle it right, there's a lot of money in the old boy. I know damn well how valuable these bones are and I'm going to swap them for a bundle."

Cheap words. But he didn't have a cheap voice. Or a cheap face. The way he talked, the way he moved, it was like an echo of all the quick clever students I'd dealt with at the museum.

"I should think . . ." I began.

"Jimmy! Jimmy, where the hell are you? Jimmy!"

The loud angry shout shocked both of us.

He snatched the skull out of my hands and grabbed up the gym bag.

"Be careful!" I cried. "Don't drop it, for God's sake!"

He didn't bother to answer. He plumped the skull into the bag, began to zip it shut.

The door burst open behind us and we both turned to face it.

"So there you are. What the hell are you up to, Jimmy?"

Jimmy, his face tight and angry, held the gym bag close to his chest. "What do you want, Dan?"

The newcomer, Dan, loomed in the doorway. He was a good deal bigger than Jimmy. A man, not a boy. And he looked out of place in that narrow basement room with its single shabby cot and shelves of orange crates. His suit was a grey pinstripe and it fitted him superbly. Everything about him commanded attention.

Especially his face.

Some faces, once seen, stay with you always. I would know him where ever we met again. I would not forget his face, deepset black eyes, straight black brows drawn now in a tight frown, a thin tough mouth, high sharp-angled cheeks. In a different age, in a faraway country, it would have been the face of a warlord.

He looked from Jimmy to me. His eyes rested on me for a long moment, bold appraising eyes.

"What's going on?" Dan's voice was as compelling as his face; husky, abrasive, insistent.

Jimmy edged back a step. "How did you know we were here?"

"Sammy Ching," Dan answered. "He passed the two of you. He was curious enough to turn and watch—and when he saw you bring her here, he called me." His eyes slid back to me, then, unexpectedly, he grinned, a good-humoured lively grin. He nodded slowly. "I can understand Sammy's interest, but," and the laughter left his voice, "this isn't the place, Jimmy. I would have damn well thought you would know better. To bring a woman to the basement of a family association," he shook his head again, "that won't do. And it isn't even the Lee family association!"

"Look, Dan, it isn't what you think," Jimmy objected. "I needed a place that was empty and Jack Wong went to visit his son today so I knew no one was here. Besides, it isn't any of your damn business, anyway."

Dan looked at Jimmy intently. "Why else would you bring a woman here?"

"Now, just a minute . . ." I began angrily.

"Look, Dan, it isn't . . ."

But Jimmy never finished. His eyes widened. I saw fear and shock move in his eyes. For an instant, he stared, his mouth still open, then, so quickly that all of us were taken unawares, his hand moved, he grabbed up the heavy lantern-shaped flashlight and threw it hard and straight toward the single low-watt bulb that hung from an electrical cord in the centre of the ceiling. In the last instant before the flashlight smashed into the bulb and it chattered in a fiery crackle, I half-turned toward the door and saw them, two of them, black leather jackets, tight dirty Levis, broad flat empty old-young faces, saw them and recognized danger.

THREE

The flashlight landed on its side, its bright wide beam parallel to the floor, affording one sharp spot of light against the back wall and a dim illumination for the rest of the room. Everyone moved at once in an ominous silence, the only sounds a sharply indrawn breath, the scuff of shoes, the slither of leather.

I knew what they wanted. And I didn't care how Jimmy talked about bundles of cash, my immediate instinctive reaction was that Peking Man was better off in his hands.

I was moving, too, scrambling sideways toward the tool bench. Scarcely able to make it out in the gloom, I remembered the neatly hung tools—and a claw hammer at the near end.

Everybody was moving, although Dan was slowest. I guessed that he had no idea of the contents of that gym bag. His head swung from the thugs toward Jimmy then back to the two who were almost upon him now.

I yanked the hammer free. As I turned back, I saw Jimmy ducking down, yanking up that shabby cot, thrusting it forward. Dan took it, hesitated, then swung it straight up. For an instant, I was delighted. Both of them, I thought, he's taken on both of them. I looked around, hoping Jimmy would take this chance, maybe the only chance, to slip past them and run out the door. Then perhaps Dan and I . . .

I was holding the hammer up, waiting, and realized with a sick sense of shock that Dan hadn't got both of them—and that Jimmy was scrambling toward the back of the room! Why wasn't he running for the door? Why on earth would he turn that way, a brick wall ahead of him, the sad row of orange-crate shelves to his left, the toolbench to his right?

Then I stopped worrying about Jimmy because the cot had caught only one of the attackers. The shorter heavier thug sidestepped and moved into Dan.

Now there was noise, lots of it, a strange screeching like old metal, the horrid thump of fists on flesh, breathless harsh grunts of pain and an agonized yelp when my hammer whanged into the shorter thug's shoulder—he'd moved his head at the last minute. I must have numbed him good because he staggered into the tool bench, slumped over it for an instant, then swung around and landed a vicious kick that caught me in the thigh and I yelped, too, and flew backwards and brought up painfully against the wall then crumpled to the floor. Someone toppled to the floor near me, swearing in a low monotonous voice. He landed on the flashlight, there was a crackling sound and it was abruptly absolutely dark. I heard scuffling sounds, a dull thump, a sickening crack. Someone ran heavily. Then a cold damp current of air swept me and it was suddenly quiet. Deathly quiet.

"Jimmy?" My voice wavered.

No one answered, no one moved. There was nothing but that odd eddy of air, cold, dank and smelling of earth and age.

"Dan?" My voice was sharp now, frightened. Damn yes, I was frightened. Who was in that cold cellar with me? Who lay on that hard-packed earthen floor? For I was sure that I wasn't alone.

A rustle, a groggy moan of pain.

What if Jimmy and Dan were both gone? What if they had deserted me down here, damn them, and that moan came from one of those toughs?

It was obviously everybody for himself and I had better see to Ellen before the moaner came to.

I was on my hands and knees now, my right leg still throbbing from that kick. Cautiously, I began to get up, reaching out to the wall for support.

"Uhh." Someone moved not far from me.

I began to limp quietly, sliding my hand along the wall. I touched the doorframe. The hall lay just ahead of me. I could feel my way to the stairs and get up and out of this nightmare.

"Uhh."

I hesitated by the door. It might be Jimmy lying there, moaning. Or Dan. And what if somewhere in this dark eerily cold cellar lay the gym bag with Peking Man's skull stuffed inside?

Down that hall lay safety. Or, at least, a chance at it.

"Uhh."

I took a step nearer the door. Why should I care who moaned? No one was a friend of mine. Then, almost angrily, I turned away from the doorframe and began, step by cautious step, to move toward the centre of the room and whoever lay there. One step, another, then I was falling, yanked off my feet by the hand that had closed roughly around my ankle. I went down heavily, landing on my sore right hip.

"Ouch!" I yelled.

"Oh, oh sorry. Sorry," he said muzzily, "didn't know it was you." Letting go as suddenly as he had grabbed, he began to struggle to get up. "Jimmy, hey Jimmy!" and his voice was stronger.

The silence must have hit him as it had me. It was such a cold empty silence.

"Goddammit Jimmy, where are you?" Harshly, he turned on me. "Where is he? What's happened? Where did they go?"

"If I knew," I said drily, "you would be among the first to hear."

He was on his feet now. I couldn't see him but he was close

30

to me, so close I could hear him breathe. "Don't try to be funny. What's happened to Jimmy?"

He didn't ask if I was all right or put out a hand to help me up. No, he loomed above me in the utter darkness and yelled about Jimmy.

"Why on earth do you care?" I demanded pettishly. "He wasn't so very damn glad to see you, was he? And you don't even know what it's all about, do you?"

He did pull me up then, but not nicely. His big hand swung down, found my elbow and hauled me up like a sack of meal.

"But you do know." His voice was almost ugly. "And you're going to tell me!"

I tried to pull away from him. "Why should I tell you anything at all?"

"Because Jimmy's my brother."

"Oh."

His hand hurt my arm. But I wasn't mad any more. I understood now why Dan had fought even though he didn't know what the gym bag held. He didn't know why toughs trailed his brother—and what I was going to tell him wouldn't help much. It would only give him more reason to fear for his brother.

"Let go," I said quietly. "I'll tell you what I know. But it isn't much, isn't enough. And I'm sorry he's your brother. I didn't know."

His hand fell away from me. "Where did they go? Did they get Jimmy? Hurt him?"

"I don't know," I answered uncertainly. "Everything happened so quickly. I saw Jimmy push the cot at you and then I thought, when you swung it at those two, that Jimmy would try to get to the door. But he didn't. He turned toward the back wall. Then I lost track of him. I'd found a hammer and

31

taken a swing at one of the toughs but, unfortunately, I missed his head. He kicked me and the next thing I knew the middle of the room was erupting, then the light went out." I shrugged. "That's all I know. It was dark and, suddenly, quiet."

"They had to go somewhere," Dan muttered. "Here," and he flicked a lighter and there was a tiny quivering tongue of flame. He held it up and the flame danced and promptly went out. He clicked the lighter again and this time shielded the wick.

We looked around and, even in that wavering uncertain light that more softened than dispelled the gloom, we both saw the darker splotch of blackness in the wall where the cot had stood. Saw and half understood that cold damp eddy of air, saw and cautiously moved nearer.

It was cleverly done, cleverly, painstakingly, artfully done. Bricks had been split then mounted in a wood frame and fitted into the wall. Closed, the squat square door merged into the brick wall. Opened, it revealed a low entryway. Dan knelt, still protecting his tint flare of light from the cool damp air that flowed into the cellar.

"I'll be dammed," he said softly.

He poked his head and shoulders into the darkness, held the little light inside the opening. It immediately snuffed out. "There's a narrow space behind this wall." His voice was muffled. "I can feel air, fresher air." Then his voice was close again and I knew he had pulled back from the opening. "At some time, probably after the big earthquake in 1907, the building was rebuilt with a double wall at the cellar level, leaving room for a passageway."

The raspy click sounded again and the lighter once more burned. It cast uneven jumpy shadows that made the dark cellar seem alive with sinister movement. He turned toward me and I wished I could see his face more clearly. His voice was strong, reassuring. "It has to be a way out. We know that. Jimmy and those guys must have gone this way. Look, do you want to wait here . . ."

His voice trailed off. I understood his dilemma. He didn't want to leave me here. How could he trust me to stay until he returned? And, he needed me to find out what was going on. However, he couldn't insist that I follow him blindly to who knew what.

"I'll come along." I had no intention of remaining in that unlighted room by myself. He might not be my champion, but he was certainly better than being alone. Under the circumstances.

He went first, taking the lighter with him, of course, and the cellar was suddenly much darker. It took me a moment in the scant light to find my purse and to take one last hopeful look around for that gym bag. He was back in the cellar, wary and suspicious, when I didn't come.

"Ready?"

"I'm right behind you."

The opening was low, beneath the bulletin board that had hung over the cot. I stooped and stepped into the narrow passageway. We had to turn sideways to move. I kept close behind him. I wondered how many years this passageway had existed—and for what purpose? It was bricked underfoot unlike the cellar floor. The bricks were uneven, more like cobbles, and slick. In the wavering light I could see a darkish spread of fungus on the wall near my face and I wondered if the whole passageway was coated and slimy. I shivered and kept right behind Dan. So near, in fact, that I bumped him good when he stopped suddenly.

"Shhh!" he warned.

I stood on one foot, massaging my right ankle where it had

come up under his heel and trying to listen over the sudden uneven thumping of my heart.

Then I heard it, too. A skittery rustle just ahead. We waited. The sound came again, seemed louder now that we listened for it.

Dan bent low, held the lighter forward.

Tiny eyes glittered at us. A sleek rat, his fur ghostly in the dark, watched us then tentatively nosed a step nearer.

Dan stamped his foot. grey fur flashed and was gone.

"Just a rat," he said easily. "Come on."

Just a rat. Damn, I wanted out!

We must have walked almost fifty yards with just space enough to squeeze between the two brick walls when the passageway ended at the foot of a narrow wooden stairway, the treads not more than a foot in width. We could see a square of light not too far above.

Dan climbed up first and looked out cautiously then gestured for me to follow. We stepped out into a ground-floor entryway. This small squat door was a movable piece of panelling and would, like its counterpart in the cellar, be well disguised when closed.

Dan gently touched a finger to my lips, but he didn't need to caution me for I, too, heard the sounds, an intermittent clicking noise, the low indistinguishable mutter of voices, then, abruptly, a loud whoop of laughter.

Dan raised his head and I realized the sounds came from upstairs. A stairway, scarcely visible in the dim light, twisted upward, out of sight.

I watched Dan's face, what I could see of it in the faint light that seeped through the narrow opening of a door not too far from us that stood ajar. Now he put a finger to his own lips, then nodded for me to follow him. He began to step, softly as a cat, toward that opened door.

I didn't know why he moved so quietly, what threat he recognized, but I tiptoed, too. We were almost to the door, his hand was reaching out for the knob, when we heard the sharp click of shoes on asphalt.

Dan looked back toward the stairs, then again at the door—and the footsteps came nearer.

Dan's arm swung around me and he almost carried me as he moved us quickly to the side of the door where we would be hidden when the door opened.

The steps came close then abruptly stopped and I knew someone stood just past that partially-opened door, stood and listened as we did.

Seconds passed, interminable seconds. Upstairs the clicking sounds continued and the soft murmur of voices. I could hear the feather-light sound of Dan's breath.

The door began to open, slowly, so slowly. It swung back against us and someone walked lightly into the room.

I heard a shocked mutter and running feet. The hidden door was still open!

That's when Dan won my confidence. He didn't hesitate. He didn't wait too long or move too soon. Grabbing my arm, he edged us around the door and then we were dashing out the open door. I just glimpsed a figure peering into the passageway. Hearing us, he whirled around, shouted. Answering shouts came down the stairwell and, as we jumped into the street, we heard the running thump of feet coming down the stairs.

"Run like hell!" Dan ordered.

FOUR

We reached the end of the street and tumbled out into Grant Avenue and were immediately caught up in the flow of restaurant goers and sightseers.

Huge Chinese characters, incomprehensible to me, flickered in brilliant neon on both sides of the street. Little shops offered candy, art goods, paintings, ivories and every other doorway led to a restaurant.

We merged into the stream of unhurried pedestrians and didn't look back when we heard our pursuers reach Grant. Dan held my elbow and hurried us straight ahead for another block. Once across the intersection, we ducked into the alcove of a shop which was shuttered for the night.

It was light enough in that alcove for us to see each other plainly and I was struck once again by the character and force in his face. I could well see that he and Jimmy were brothers, though Jimmy's face was much more gentle and diffident.

I could also see that Dan's right cheek was beginning to swell.

"Does it hurt?"

"Hurt?"

"Your face."

"Oh, that. No. Not much. Son of a bitch hit me a good one." His voice was grim. "I'd like to know why. I'd like to know a hell of a lot. I'll start with you. Who are you? Why were you with Jimmy? What the hell's happening?"

"I'm Ellen Christie. I was with Jimmy because he wanted to show something to me. I'll try to tell you as much as I

36

know, but, first, I have some questions of my own. Who are you? Where did that passageway come out? And, why did we have to run?"

His face was immobile for a long moment then his mouth spread in a wide grin. His very attractive mouth.

"Have you ever spent much time in Chinatown?"

I shook my head. "Lunch. Once."

"Tonight should make up for that. To begin with, we walked through a secret passageway. Right?"

I nodded.

"Every Chinese will tell you there's no truth to the old tales about Chinatown being honeycombed with tunnels. That's just the old hokey anti-Chinese newspaper tong-war publicity. I grew up three blocks from here and I would have told you there wasn't a tunnel in town. I would have laughed at the idea of hidden passageways, too, which goes to show that nobody knows everything. As for where it came out," he laughed, "that's what the tabloids like to call a 'gambling den' and we ran because they don't like strangers dropping in. Especially strangers popping in through what is obviously their pet exit."

"I see."

"And I'm Dan Lee. A lawyer by trade. I have a little brother named Jimmy." The good humour left his voice. "And I'm afraid he's in trouble."

I nodded slowly. "Trouble—and danger," I said sombrely. "I don't know how or where but somehow he's come up with an incredibly valuable collection of fossils and I'm afraid he's out to sell to the highest bidder."

Dan bent closer as if to hear better. "He's come up with what?"

"Fossils. At least one fossil, and I'm guessing he has them all." I hesitated, then plunged ahead. "I won't swear to it because scientists won't just from a look and, besides, I'm no expert on Sinanthropus, but he showed me a skull—and it's Peking Man. I know it is. Damn, I just know it is!"

Dan took a deep breath, folded his arms and stared down at me. "Miss Christie . . ."

"Ellen," I interrupted.

"All right, Ellen. But, you lose me. Are you trying to say those toughs were after a skull? An old fossilized skull?"

"Not just any old skull," I said impatiently. "It's Peking Man."

Dan just shrugged and it finally came clear to me that the name meant nothing to him.

It's hard sometimes to realize that intelligent well-educated people may not know a thing about our own particular specialty. I probably wouldn't know a tort from a torte except my father is a smalltown lawyer, oil and gas, civil trials and probate his areas.

I just stood there for a moment, uncertain how to begin.

"Bone, skull, whatever," he said, "you think those toughs were out to take it away from Jimmy? But that he has as much right to it as anybody?"

"The first, yes. The second, well, that's anybody's guess. I'd say whoever has the bones in hand is in a position of strength, either to claim a reward or to sell them."

Dan nodded. "Then, if I can't find Jimmy," and he paused and I knew he was afraid for his brother.

"If you can't find him," I repeated soberly.

"Then I'd better get the police."

I looked out onto Grant Avenue, at the cheerful pedestrians enjoying the colour of an exotic enclave. All kinds of people passed by and none of them looked dangerous. But that didn't mean much. That red-haired woman looking up at the curly-haired sailor or that impassive Navajo staring into a shop window or that middle-aged paunchy man in the ill-fitting suit trying to keep up with his very young companion, what would they do for a hundred thousand dollars? Or, perhaps, for two hundred thousand dollars? Multiply them by all the people in San Francisco who read newspapers. Out of these thousands of people, some of them would know who Peking Man was and would know quite well how much he was worth.

And some people will go to great extremes for money.

"It would be a sensation in the newspapers," I said slowly.

"Oh, there are muggings, that kind of thing . . ." he began.

I shook my head. "No. Don't you see, if you go to the police, they will want to know why somebody is after Jimmy. Some reporter would pick it up, that Jimmy had what looked to be a skull of Peking Man . . . and that would tear it."

He was sceptical. "Look, Miss . . . Ellen, I gather you know something about fossils, that this is your thing, but, you know, the average person isn't much interested in dry scientific . . ."

"Right," I interrupted, "but the average guy likes price tags. And entrepreneurs get really turned on by bundles of dollars. Like one hundred thousand dollars. Maybe up to half-a-million."

His head jerked up as if I'd slapped him. I finally had his attention.

"Oh." He thought about it. "And the bones are up for grabs? Whoever has them can sell them? Is that what you mean?"

I nodded.

"So if this broke in the newspapers, then anybody in San Francisco who could find Jimmy and get the bones . . . by whatever means . . . would be in line for the money?"

I nodded again.

"Damn," he said softly. Then, lawyerlike, he came back to ownership. "They must belong to somebody."

I answered uncertainly, "The bones belonged to the Peking Union Medical College a long time ago. Beyond that, they should belong to the Peoples' Republic of China." I rubbed at my cheek. "I'm not sure on it, but I think, from what I've read, that the United States government has indicated unofficially that it would like to see the bones, if recovered in the United States, returned to mainland China. I do know the FBI joined in the search several years ago when it was rumoured that the bones had come to light in New York."

"But the FBI couldn't find them?"

"No."

"But if the bones do turn up then there will be several lots on Jimmy's tail, including the FBI and mainland Chinese agents?"

"Yes," I agreed. "Plus, of course, any local supporters of Nationalist China."

"God yes," he replied. "There are a lot of them." He sighed. "This is no time to explain Chinatown's ties to Taiwan but you can take my word for it that there are thousands of older Chinese who have spent years supporting Taiwan because they thought it was the right role for all good Americans. The detente between the U.S. and mainland China has left a lot of them floundering between banks. Many of the younger Chinese are all for mainland China." He frowned. "Why should Taiwan want the bones? Or mainland China either?"

He still didn't see Peking Man for what he was.

I could have talked for hours. I did talk furiously for a few minutes.

"Those fossil bones are the earliest, the very earliest, finds

40

of man in China. Moreover, they are definitely ancestral to today's Chinese. So, the Chinese have very strong feelings that these fossils are rightfully theirs even aside from the fact that they were found in China."

"Okay," Dan rejoined, "ancestor worship on a grand scale. But still . . ."

"Even more important to all anthropologists is the fact that no group of fossil bones anywhere in the word matches these for containing the bones of so many individuals from a single population. The total collection included bones from about forty persons.

"In addition, the study of fossils never stops, and casts, which were made of Peking Man and which survive today, can never match the real thing so . . ."

He held up his hands, staving off the words. "All right. I'll take it on faith. Somebody somewhere will ante up to a half-million," and he shook his head wonderingly, "for these bones. But how can Jimmy Lee get in touch with the right man?"

I shrugged. "I don't know." Then the word struck me, turned itself inside out, and I clutched Dan's sleeve and said excitedly, "Maybe that's it, maybe that explains the thugs. Maybe Jimmy tried to sell the bones but he tried the 'wrong' man, somebody who decided it would be easy to grab the bones and run. Or . . ." I hesitated, but it was another real possibility, "or maybe Jimmy lifted them and someone's out to get them back."

Dan was quiet for a long moment and I wondered if I had offended him. But he spoke consideringly, "I don't suppose I can even say about my own brother when it comes to a half-million dollars, but Jimmy's never really cared about money. I don't think he'd steal anything. He must have come by the fossils honestly."

I remembered that quick young voice, telling me how he was going to cash in on Peking Man.

But Dan was still talking. "You see, Jimmy's always been one of those damn-fool kids who's hung up on some cause or other." Dan's voice hardened. "If Jimmy'd had to work his way through college, maybe he wouldn't feel so soft about guys on welfare. I earned every penny of my way. I made a mistake when I gave Jimmy money for college, but I wanted him to have it easier than the rest of us did. Maybe it gave him too much time. All he's done is march for this 'wrong' and picket for something else and work for nothing to try and help the immigrants. I keep telling him that they'll make it okay. It doesn't hurt people to have to work . . ."

"What if they can't get jobs?" I asked quietly.

He turned on me. "So you're one of them, too. Everybody wants a job handed to them on a platter. It's all this permissive crap in the colleges." He stopped and sighed. When he spoke again, his voice was tired, expressionless. "I hadn't seen Jimmy for six months until tonight."

I wanted to tell him that I understood. Because I did. I was between him and Jimmy in age, able to see both worlds, perhaps better than either of them. Dan had, obviously, hauled himself up by bootstraps. Jimmy thought bootstraps suspect in a world where nothing held to its outward reality.

"Why hadn't you seen him?"

"He dropped out of school."

A world of unhappiness and accusation and sheer dismay in his voice.

"What's he been doing?"

"Living in a damn commune." He paused then said grudgingly, "Well, I guess that's not quite fair. He's got a job with a kind of shoestring social agency and he's rented an apartment and gone around and picked up these kids off the street; you know, drop-outs, that kind, and he helps them get jobs. A lot of them are new kids, you know, fresh from Hong Kong and they can't speak English very well. Jimmy's started some classes, the hip kind of thing to pull in these kids who won't go to the more straight classes."

"I don't believe," I said softly, "that I would be angry with Jimmy." I began to have some idea why Jimmy would want money.

"He should have finished school," Dan said stubbornly. "Eighteen hours to go and he drops out."

"He'll go back."

"Now there's this mess. Tough guys after him. But if I call the cops for help, then half San Francisco may be looking for him."

"But, if we don't go to the police," I said unhappily, "then how can we ever hope to find him?"

"We?" he repeated.

I looked up at him, at his darkly handsome face dimly seen in the shadowy shop entry.

"Oh yes," I said firmly. "If you'll remember, I was invited in. And I'm in it to stay until we find Jimmy."

And, of course, I thought to myself, until we find Peking Man.

FIVE

Jimmy's motorcycle was gone from the alley. We stood uncertainly by the rack of garbage pails.

"He must have got away from them," Dan said. "So, I guess the first place to look for him is his apartment. It isn't listed so those toughs wouldn't go there."

It was a tenement only a couple of blocks off Grant Avenue, a weary down-at-heels building, windows so grimed with dirt they were opaque, sightless eyes in a crumbling facade. The entry door hung loosely on its hinges and wouldn't latch.

Dan held the door for me and I stepped into the cramped hallway. A single low-watt bulb dangled from a cord.

You are sometimes intensely aware of other people, in a packed lecture hall, at a sold-out movie theatre, wedged into an elevator during the morning rush.

Standing in that small linoleum-floored entryway, waiting while Dan bent to check the boxes, I sensed a multitude of people near, smelled damp washes, cabbage and fish, and heard an unceasing rustle and creak of movement, the dull mumble of radios and televisions, footsteps, the rattle of water pipes, a baby's tired cry.

Behind us, the outer door creaked slowly in and an older, heavy-set man shrugged past, ignoring us, not so much hostile as indifferent. He climbed the stairs and it was painful to watch. He climbed slowly, so slowly, with such weariness. It was more than exhaustion. Every heavy footfall thumped dully on the stairs. On his way home but nothing to look for-

44

ward to. Not tonight. Or tomorrow. Or forever. Tired and drained, defeated and despairing.

Dan and I watched him climb, so slowly, so agonizingly slowly. And around us, surrounding us, pressing on us, was the rustle and breath of people.

"Sometimes," Dan said with no expression in his voice, "three families will share one kitchen. There will be only one toilet on each floor. Half the time, the toilets don't work and need a pan of water to flush. The water's cold. No hot water. And no heat."

The entry door swung in again. An elderly woman squinted at us, then smiled shyly and slipped by to hurry up the stairs, clutching a bundle with tip ends of cloth straggling loose.

"Just a little night work. Hell, this place spooks me. C'mon, Ellen, this way," and he took my elbow and we started up the stairs.

"Night work?"

"The old lady."

"What do you mean?"

"It's the old garment racket. Chinatown has a bunch of little factories that do piecework for the downtown factories. Problem is, too many Chinatown shops so the big outfits downtown chivvy down the price until the ladies that sew end up making thirty, forty, fifty cents an hour. Lots of them work all day and still have to bring work home at night."

We were at the landing, starting up the second flight of steps. Narrow steps these, uncarpeted, warped, slanting toward the banister.

Again, the only light came from a single hanging bulb. On the second floor, Dan turned toward the back of the building and I followed. I could smell rice cooking and hear a small child singing. Two men waited outside a doorway midway down the hall. We skirted past them and their heads turned to watch us. We stopped at the last door.

Dan knocked.

A teenage boy opened the door. The room beyond was dim, the only light spreading in flickering halftones from the black-and-white television set against the opposite wall. Not that the wall was far away. The room was diminutive, ten feet by twelve perhaps, and at first glance seemed full of people.

Dan was asking the boy about Jimmy and I sorted out the dim figures, two on a narrow couch against the wall, the other four lounging on the floor. Six boys.

"No, no, Jimmy not here. He late."

A heavier boy pushed up slowly from the couch, walked with a swagger to the door.

"You looking for Jimmy?" It wasn't the words, it was his tone. I could almost feel Dan's hackles rise.

"Yeah, buddy. Has he been here tonight?"

The boy shrugged.

I touched Dan's arm before he could answer.

"Please," I said, "we're hoping you can help us. Jimmy was supposed to meet us but he didn't come. Has he been here, oh, in the last hour or so?"

The boy's dark eyes moved slowly to me. He didn't smile. His eyes were cold and angry, but I knew the anger wasn't at me. He had been angry for a long time. Slowly, he shook his head. "No. No, he hasn't been here."

A door opened down the hallway. A woman stepped out, carrying a saucepan. A little girl followed close behind her.

"If Jimmy comes, please tell him that Ellen and his brother are looking for him. That we need to talk to him. That we want . . . to help him."

"Brother?" the boy repeated. "I didn't know Jimmy had a brother."

"He does," Dan said shortly. "Tell him I came. And, tell him he'd damn well better call me, the mess he's in."

I could have strangled Dan. But, it was too late.

The boy's angry eyes swung back to Dan. Even though Dan was much the bigger, I was afraid for an instant. The boy's mouth curled a little.

"Tell him yourself," he said softly and the door slammed in our faces, quivering in its frame.

"Goddam smart ass, I'll . . ."

"No," I said sharply.

Dan's fist, raised to pound on the door, slowly dropped to his side. He glared at me then shook his head wearily. "Sorry, Ellen. Sorry. You're right. Damn dumb. I know better. Like the old lawyer said, honey catches flies every time. It's just . . ." he rubbed the side of his face tiredly, "it's just that I'm so damn sick of smart mouth kids. All right, I blew it. Let's go. I can't think here."

As we started down the stairs, he said reassuringly, "I'll find Jimmy. Don't worry about that. I know Chinatown."

How many people in Chinatown, I wondered. I'd read the figure once. Thirty-five, forty thousand people, all crowded into a twenty-four block area. Lots of hiding places down there.

But Dan said it once again when we reached the sidewalk. Both of us welcomed the cold damp air, the feeling of space and freedom, welcomed it but our eyes avoided saying so.

"We'll find him," Dan insisted.

Half-an-hour later even Dan was losing confidence. We were at the public phone booth on the sidewalk next to Old St Mary's, that distinctive booth that is shaped like a pagoda, red-roofed with uptilted eaves. I stood by as Dan made call after call, Jimmy's old roommate in Berkeley, Dan and Jimmy's brothers, Pete and Eddie, their sisters, Ruth and

Janet, a couple of Jimmy's best friends from high school.

Dan made one last call.

"Mother? Hi, Dan here. How's everything . . . mmm . . . no, no, I hadn't heard that . . . well, that's great, a little girl, huh? . . . I know, yeah, it's been too long . . . no . . . sure thing, I'll try Sunday . . . hey, Mother, have you been home all evening? . . . no, no special reason, just wanted to talk to you, see how you are . . . sure . . . okay . . . night."

He stepped outside the booth and, when he looked at me, I could see the fear in his eyes. "Nobody's seen him, nobody's talked to him." He frowned. "I don't like it. Usually, if one of us gets in a tight, well, he turns to somebody in the family. That's the way it is. I'm afraid . . ." Grimly, he stepped back into the booth and began to call the hospitals.

But Jimmy, if he was hurt, was not in a hospital.

Then Dan was angry again. "When I get my hands on him, I'll knock some sense into his head."

I understood that kind of anger. Dan wanted so badly for his little brother to be all right.

But Jimmy didn't want anyone, family or friends, to know where he was. Not if my guess was right. And I was guessing that he was lying low, trying to figure out how to sell his bonanza. So Jimmy was not going to be easy to find.

But maybe we could approach it another way. If we could find out where Jimmy got the bones, we might get close to him.

"Dan, we need to . . ."

"Ellen, where do you suppose . . ."

I finished it for him. ". . . Jimmy got the skull?"

"And where are the rest of the bones?" Dan asked. "Didn't you say the whole collection included the bones of about forty people? Why, that would . . ."

I shook my head. "Just bits and pieces, Dan. We aren't

talking about a big mass of bones. Nothing like forty complete skeletons. No complete skeleton, of course, was ever found. These fossils had been crushed and covered by falling cave rocks and buried under tons of material for a half-million years, perhaps longer if some recent discoveries in Africa are accurately dated. The collection was mostly teeth, lots of teeth, parts of jawbones, upper armbones, wrist bones, pieces of crania, several skulls. The whole lot could be put in an ordinary size suitcase."

"A suitcase, huh? So they're probably just sitting around in a box somewhere."

"Somewhere."

"It shouldn't be too hard," Dan said hopefully. "What we need to do is find out where Jimmy's been, what he's been up to the last few days. He can't have had the fossils long."

I nodded. "He was so excited when he came to my apartment." And I began to be excited. "You're right, Dan. That's the way it must be. He must have come across the fossils today or yesterday!"

"Okay, Ellen, now we know what to do."

"If you haven't seen him for six months, how can you have any idea where to start?" I protested.

Dan smiled. "I may not have seen him, but I know what he's been doing. I'm the eldest brother."

"The eldest brother?"

He nodded, started to speak, paused, shook his head a little. "You have a lot to learn about Chinese."

We had started to walk now and he was, once again, guiding me, his hand firm on my elbow.

When we stopped for a traffic light, I asked mildly, "Where to now?"

"Hmm? Oh, I'm going to take you home."

The light changed but I didn't move. He started to go then

stopped and looked down at me in surprise. "Did you think we were going to roam Grant all night?" and I heard the light teasing note in his voice and, suddenly again for the first time in so many years, I thought of Bill. Bill had been shorter, stockier, a flaming redhead, but there was always a touch of laughter in his voice.

"Ellen?"

"Sorry," I said quickly, "I was thinking of . . . something else." I began to move, we crossed and made it before the light turned red. "Why are you taking me home?"

"We've done all we can do tonight. What we need to do is nose around Chinatown tomorrow, find out who Jimmy's seen lately."

We turned onto Clay, walked down to Portsmouth Square. Firecrackers sputtered in the park and the lights from the ferris wheel, set up for the Chinese New Year festivities, moved in a red and green and white circle as we passed. We crossed Kearney and Dan found a cab for me in front of the Holiday Inn.

He opened the cab door, helped me in, bent to give my address to the driver. In the light from the street lamp, his hair gleamed softly black and I was fascinated once again by the angles of his face, the sense of strength and power.

"I'll call you in the morning." Then he stepped back and the cab pulled away.

Who was Dan Lee to tell me to wait his call? No asking, no co-planning. I would await his call, of course, because he was my only link to Peking Man. Not for any other reason.

SIX

He didn't call the next morning.

He came.

As I let him in, I asked a little dryly, "What if I hadn't been here?" I had already called the office, taken a day of vacation, claiming unexpected company.

He was already seated, opening his attache case to pull out a yellow legal pad. He lifted his dark head, "I said I'd call." The implication was clear. I would, of course, be awaiting his call so naturally I would be home. "I decided to come on over. We need to go at this logically."

"Oh yes," I agreed. "That's always a good idea."

He heard the laughter in my voice and, after a pause, his wide grin answered my own.

He leaned back on my couch and it suddenly looked small. "If the bones are the focus of this thing, then I need to know more about them. How they could be in San Francisco. How Jimmy might have come across them."

I, too, had had some long thoughts about Peking Man and I showed Dan the books scattered across the coffee table with markers pinpointing the relevant passages. I left him poring over a history of Peking Man while I excused myself to go and dress.

When I returned, wearing my newest pants suit, an emerald green wool, he was scratching notes onto his legal pad and he said, without looking up, "You mean the guy announced a brand new species of man on the basis of one tooth?"

I knew that he was reading about Davidson Black, the Canadian anthropologist who taught anatomy at the Peking Union Medical College in the 1920s and 1930s. Black spent his free time studying fossils and in 1927, on the basis of a single tooth excavated at Chou Kou Tien, a town some thirty miles southwest of Peking, he announced to the world the discovery of a heretofore unknown hominid, Sinanthropus pekinensis, Chinese man from Peking.

"Right. But it sounds more daring than it actually was. As a matter of fact, most fossil remains are teeth and it is fantastic what a paleontologist can tell you from a single tooth. Everything about teeth has been analyzed and they can be identified and differentiated on the basis of the forms of cusps, roots, crests and crevices, on the kinds of grooving and enamel structure. There are quite distinct patterns in teeth that are unmistakably different, for one example, from the other primates. In apes, the dental arcade has parallel sides. In man, it is parabolic. In apes, the molars are longer than they are wide. In men, the molars are wider than they are long. In apes . . ."

He was holding up his hand. "Okay, so one tooth tipped them off to a new man. Then they went and dug up more of him, right?"

I nodded.

He riffled on a few more pages. "How did the stuff get lost?" He stopped. "On a ship?"

"That's an old book, a general history of famous fossils. It was thought, shortly after World War II, that the bones had been shipped out of China on the S.S. *President Harrison* and had gone down when she sank, but it was later learned that the bones never reached the ship."

I had brought in a tray with coffee and I pushed some books aside to put it down, then I joined him on the couch, poured us each a cup, and tried to get it all straight in my mind.

"You have to go back a long way," I explained. "To November of 1941. Americans and especially the Americans at the Peking Union Medical College were getting nervous, afraid Japan's war with China was going to expand to include the United States. Finally, it was decided to send the fossils to the United States. They were packed in two white marine footlockers and loaded on a train for Tientsin, there to be shipped on the S.S. *President Harrison*. But time had run out. The train reached Camp Holcomb, a marine installation, on December 8. That was December 7 American time and the Japanese attacked Pearl Harbor that morning and America was in the war. The Japanese immediately arrested all Americans, including the Marines.

"Now, it's from this point that no one knows what happened to the fossils. There are lots of theories:

"The Japanese soldiers, looting the marine camp, ripped open the footlockers and, not knowing the value of the bones, just tossed the fossils away.

"A Japanese soldier recognized the fossils for what they were and took them. Now, this gives scope for a lot of possibilities. The soldier kept them throughout the war and got back to Japan and has had them hidden there ever since. Or, he sold them to some Chinese who has also kept them hidden. Or he hid them in China and they're still undiscovered.

"A variation on this theme is that one of the American marines latched on to them. This was possible because the fossils were packed in marine footlockers and, after they were captured, the marines in prison camp later received some of their footlockers. According to this theory, a marine, possibly one who had worked around the Peking Union Medical College and knew the value of the bones, managed to keep them hidden while a prisoner and after the war smuggled them into the United States. This theory would account for the mysterious woman who lives somewhere on the East Coast who has made a couple of abortive attempts to sell what she claims are the fossils, brought home after the war by her husband."

Dan brought me up sharply. "You mean the bones have actually surfaced in the United States?"

I turned my hands palm up. "Who knows? There's a well-known Chicago businessman, Christopher Janus, who's been hunting for the fossils ever since he visited Red China and felt the Chinese were asking ever so subtly for his help in recovering the fossils. Janus has even offered one hundred and fifty thousand dollars for the bones, and that's brought him some action."

I took a sip of the coffee. I'm partial to coffee and chicory. Dan took a taste, looked at his mug curiously, took another.

"Like it?"

"Yeah. Something a little extra, huh?"

"Chicory."

"You talk that way, too."

I shook my head.

He smiled. "I like the way you talk."

"Anyway," I said quickly, back to Bach, "money ripples the water like sharks after meat. When the word got out, and it was well publicized, that the bones were worth at least one hundred and fifty thousand, there have been a couple of responses that may be genuine."

One of them I described very briefly as there wasn't a lot to it. A Chinese businessman in New York had contacted Janus, talked knowledgably about the fossils, then backed away from any serious discussions, claiming it was too dangerous.

It was the other contact which excited everyone involved

54

in the search. A woman phoned, claimed she had the fossils, said she was the widow of a marine who had been stationed in Peking, offered to meet Janus.

"And she did, she met him in the observatory of the Empire State Building."

"Aw, come on," Dan protested.

"No, I'm serious. She came, a fairly tall dark-haired woman about forty. She showed him a photograph of this dark looking box with the lid off and in it were some bones scattered on a bed of straw. She was showing the picture when a tourist turned toward them, lifted his camera. She immediately dashed for the elevators."

"She thought it was all set up to get a picture of her?" Dan asked.

"Yes. And she wasn't having any. Janus managed to get on the same elevator with her and insisted that he hadn't arranged for her to be photographed, but she wouldn't listen and she got away from him in the street.

"The woman had contacted him at least twice since but she would never arrange a meeting, never make any of the bones available for study by an expert. But she did send him a copy of the box photograph."

I finished my coffee, leaned back. "No one has quite written her off. I mean, the picture exists. Of course, several experts have looked at it and the situation gets a little muddled because some of the bones can't be Peking Man fossils . . ."

"Why not?"

"Because some of the bones pictured were never found in the excavations."

"Oh well, then," Dan began.

"But," I interrupted softly, "there is a portion of one skull that a world-famous paleontologist has studied in blow-ups of that photograph—and he thinks it just very well may be."

Dan had been ready to strike through some of his notes. His pen stopped. But he was frowning. "Have they hunted for this woman? Checked the widows of marines who were stationed there?"

"Oh, yes. Private detectives have hunted and so has the FBI. But no one's been able to trace her."

"I don't see how she could be in Chinatown," Dan said, almost to himself.

I haven't told you all the theories and some of them are a little closer to Chinatown. A couple of years ago a man was hiking in the foothills near Sonora. He found a deserted cabin and, in it, a footlocker. With bones. It was too much to carry. He told a friend when he reached home but when they searched for the cabin a few months later and found it, there wasn't any footlocker."

"That's still a long way from Chinatown."

"Right. But let's go back to China, back to December of 1941. After the marines were taken into custody, some of the officers were permitted to stay in Peking for a week or so, under a sort of house-arrest. The Japanese were, in the beginning, very considerate of rank.

"One of the American marine officers was a doctor, William T. Foley, who is now a heart specialist in New York. Dr Foley had many Chinese friends.

"Now, according to one version of the packing up of the fossils, they were packed in marine footlockers and carried the names of Dr Foley and of Col William W. Ashurst, the commanding officer of the marine detachment in Peking. This is important because the Japanese returned the captured officers' footlockers to them in Peking.

"The colonel, who is now dead, said after the war that he did receive one footlocker full of bones and that he hid it as a prisoner but lost track of it in 1945. On the other hand, Dr Foley has said that he didn't open the footlockers that were returned to him and doesn't know if they had been opened and searched. He had four footlockers. He gave two to friends to keep for him, stored one locker at the Swiss Warehouse and another at the Pasteur Institute, both in Tientsin."

"Which lockers were the bones in?"

"The doctor has never said. Perhaps he doesn't know. In any event, nobody knows. And nobody knows what happened to any of those four lockers."

"That's not close to Chinatown," Dan said.

"There are immigrants, aren't there?"

He nodded. "About four thousand a year and they come to Chinatown. You're saying that if the lockers survived the war and if the fossils were in one of them, someone may have brought that locker to the United States—and Jimmy found out about it."

"That's possible." I refilled our mugs. "There have also been hints that the fossils might be in Formosa or in Hong Kong or Macao. You name it, it's been suggested."

Dan stared thoughtfully at his notes. Then he looked at me, just as thoughtfully.

"You're sure the skull you looked at last night was Peking Man?"

I wanted to hedge. This wasn't my specialty. How could I be expected to be positive? None of my colleagues would expect or demand an absolute answer.

But, in my heart, I was sure. The feel of the fossil, its colour, the mottled discolourations of different minerals, that bar of bone above the eye sockets; oh yes, I was sure— and I wasn't going to hedge with Dan.

"Yes," I said simply.

"All right." He accepted it. No further questions of the witness.

He checked his notes again. "This doctor . . . who were the friends he left lockers with?"

"He won't say."

Dan raised an eyebrow at that.

"I suppose," I said slowly, "that if someone in Peking has had the fossils, has kept them hidden all these years, hasn't given them to the government, I would suppose it might be very tough for him if that were revealed. The government might question his . . . loyalty." We both understood, without saying, that the present government of China demands loyalty. Would be harsh to the disloyal.

"If somebody has the bones in Peking," Dan observed, "they can't be in Chinatown."

I grinned. "That sums it up."

"There are too damn many possibilities."

"Plus some other complicating factors. I kind of hate to bring it up but you remember there were two lockers with bones?"

Dan nodded.

"Well, one footlocker held fossils discovered in what was called the Upper Cave and those were of homo sapiens and not nearly as valuable. So, when you talk about the foot-lockers, it makes a lot of difference which one you had. For example, was Col Ashurst's footlocker the one holding Peking Man or did he spend the war protecting the Upper Cave bones only to lose them toward the end of the war?"

"Oh, Lord," Dan said and he closed the legal pad and slapped it into his attache case. "I give up. The only sure thing is that nobody knows for certain what happened to the damn things—so anything's possible. Right?"

"Right."

"But maybe we can find something out from this end. Maybe, when we track down who Jimmy's talked to, who he's seen, maybe something will fit into the puzzle. We'll start at his office, his and Lily's."

"Maybe so, Dan. If we're just smart enough to see it."

SEVEN

She was angry. Her bright black eyes crackled with fury, but I knew, too, that she wasn't far from tears.

"Well, don't just stand there. Help."

The office was a shambles, file cabinets tipped over, drawers pulled out, manila folders dumped in untidy heaps on the floor. Every desk drawer had been emptied and the drawers dropped carelessly onto the scattered papers, booklets, notes, mimeograph supplies.

"Damn everthing! Why would anybody do it?"

A small plump middleaged woman, she was on her knees beside a tipped-over green filing cabinet and her hands shook as she tried to sort through manila folders, replacing loose fluttery sheets in the proper place. A stack of folders beside her began to tilt and I was able to drop down and brace the slanted slippery mass of folders and keep them from opening and spilling all their contents. As I teased them back into a secure stack, she apologized.

"I'm sorry to be so rude. I found the office like this when I came in this morning." She looked around, her face stricken. "I just can't believe anyone would do this to us." She was shaken, seeing the emptied drawers and ransacked files as an ugly flowering of viciousness.

Dan was kneeling beside us now, helping to pick up and straighten. At her words, he paused and looked around the tiny office, at the walls covered with posters, job notices, information on courses and aids for the elderly and sick and poor. "No, Lily, this isn't vandalism."

Her head jerked up, her face flushed and she fought tears. "Isn't vandalism! I'd like to know what else you could call it? Why, it's awful, it's . . ."

He reached out, patted her arm. She drew a deep breath and the tears did come then, rolling silently down her face. She used the back of a hand to try and brush them back, tiredly, as a child would.

"Don't cry, Lily," he said gently. "We'll help clean up. And, really, it isn't as bad as it looks." She started to speak but he went on, "Look around again and once you get past the first shock, you'll see how everything's been dumped— and that's all. See, they didn't tear up the files. Or spill and splatter mimeograph ink or smash anything."

She twisted her head, looked back and forth, and slowly nodded.

"There's nothing scrawled on the walls, nothing destroyed," Dan continued. "Think what a mess it could be! They could have upended the water bottle, written on the wall with those magic markers, torn and kicked and ripped everything in sight."

Lily's plump gentle face was puzzled now, some of the anger and hurt seeping away. "But what's it all about?"

"Somebody was looking for something," Dan said and his voice was grim.

Lily stared at him and her face tightened. "What's going on? You haven't come to see Jimmy in months and here you are and everything's messed up and Jimmy's late—and he's never late." Her head swung toward me. "And who are you?" Then she shook her head sharply, patted her cheeks with her hands. "I'm so sorry. That's rude, dreadfully rude! I'm just not myself."

"I'm Ellen Christie," I said quickly, "and don't apologize. I understand." I hesitated then added, "I'm a friend of

Jimmy's." But I don't think she heard me for she had turned back toward Dan, her eyes hard.

She put it baldly. "You haven't been in here, Dan, since Jimmy quit school to come to work full-time for Trouble, Inc. Why are you here today?" She looked at the paper-strewn floor. "Today of all days?"

"He should have stayed in school," Dan answered obliquely. "Should have finished his degree."

Her voice was as harsh as Dan's. "People are more important than pieces of paper."

"You can do both. You did, Lily."

Again she patted her face and her lips quivered. "I'm sorry, Dan. I don't want to quarrel with you. We've been friends for a long time." She reached out to touch his hand. "Jimmy is such a good boy. Don't be angry with him. He'll go back to school. I know he will."

Dan's hand caught hers. "Okay, Lily, we'll call a truce." He squeezed her hand gently, then dropped it. "I guess Jimmy needs all of us right now."

Her eyes were very dark and huge and frightened. "What is it, Dan? What's happened? Where's Jimmy?"

"We don't know where Jimmy is."

His voice said so much more than his words.

"I should have known something was wrong, really wrong, when he wasn't here this morning. He always comes in before me. My mother's bedridden. I see to her breakfast, settle her for the morning, before I come. Jimmy never minded, he said he liked to be out early. He always had the coffee made, had started on the list of things to be done that day . . ."

"List?" Dan interrupted.

She was impatient. "A memo, you know, so we could judge what needed to be done first. There are always so many things, so many calls, Ruth Soong's father died and she's found some kind of insurance policy, what does it mean; Frankie Wong's lost his job, the new baby needs a special formula, Frankie can't get unemployment yet; Luke Chin wants somebody to persuade his grandfather to go to the hospital, he has TB, but the old man's papers aren't any good and he's afraid; Mrs Lee's oldest boy, Yuan, didn't come home Wednesday night, she doesn't know where to look, the police aren't interested; there's a rumour the Green Door Hotel's been sold for a garage and, if it's true, what will happen to the forty-three old people who live in its rabbit-warren rooms, it's lousy but it's home and they don't have the money for better; Betty Wong hasn't been paid yet and she's been working three months in the garment factory . . ."

She stopped then said wearily, "Yeah, a memo. We put it on paper. Like that will help, huh?"

"You do help," Dan said quickly. "You do."

"The little boy at the dike." She shook herself then like a terrier flinging off rainwater. "Sure, Dan, we help. It's just that sometimes, you know, you feel like you're being buried alive. There's never enough time or money—and so many sad people. But we do help."

She was looking around once again at the shambles of the narrow crowded office. "And there's plenty to do today. I promised . . . but I have to straighten this all up first."

"That memo, the list of things Jimmy did yesterday, where would it be?"

She waved her hand at the mounds of papers and files. "It's here somewhere. Has to be. We keep the sheets for a week on a clipboard so it's easy to look back, then we slap them into a file. We always put down every place we intend to visit and, if we do something unscheduled, we add it to the list when we get back to the office."

"So yesterday's memo would show every place that Jimmy

went?" Dan's voice was deliberately uninflected but the tension was unmistakable. And Lily didn't miss it.

Slowly she nodded, her eyes intent on his face. "Why?"

He ran a hand through thick black hair and hesitated.

I didn't hesitate. I liked Lily. Liked and trusted her.

"Jimmy's come across something of value. Of great value." I didn't say what because there was no point in loading Lily with information that might endanger her. "He has as much right to it as anyone." I said it. But, was I sure?

Lily's face was an interesting mixture of curiosity and disbelief and uncertainty.

"Of great value? In Chinatown?"

Dan took it up. "Yes. Somewhere Jimmy's run across a treasure. Where else but here in Chinatown? This is where he lives and works. It has to be tied up to Chinatown." He almost smiled. "It's a . . . Chinese treasure."

She thought about it for a moment, then said crisply, "The only treasures I know about in Chinatown all belong to somebody. Ming vases, Ch'ing porcelains, jade statuettes, ivory pagodas—you don't find them lying around loose. And, I don't care what you think, Dan Lee, Jimmy isn't a thief!"

"No, I don't think he's a thief, either," Dan agreed. "But he's mixing into some very uncertain business."

"Why don't you ask Jimmy where he found this . . . treasure?"

"If we knew where he was, we would," I said quickly. "The thing about it, Lily, is that someone's after Jimmy, trying to take it away from him. We want to find him first, help him."

And recover Peking Man, I thought to myself. Put him where he belonged. In a museum. Peking Man was irreplaceable, priceless, far more important than Dan or Jimmy or I. That is what I thought.

I didn't know what Dan thought. But I don't think he

cared a hang what happened to a bundle of bones.

"Jimmy's . . . disappeared," he said gruffly. It was the first time he had put it like that.

Silence then among the three of us. Bleak silence.

"When?" Lily asked finally.

"Last night." Dan told her about the thugs and Jimmy's flight and how we hadn't been able to find any trace of him, not at his room or at friends' or among the family.

"The hospitals?" she asked.

"We checked them," Dan answered. "There's no trace of him. Anywhere."

"All right," she said quickly. "I'll give you the names of the people he's visited lately. At least, I will if we can find the memo in all this mess."

"We'll help," I offered again.

With three of us working, even though Dan and I had to be told where to put everything, it took us no more than half-an-hour to clear up the worst of the mess.

The clipboard turned up toward the end of our straightening, lying upside down beneath an overturned filing cabinet.

"Here," Lily cried, picking it up.

Dan took it, ran his finger down the sheet, nodding to himself.

"There are the visits he made Wednesday," she explained. "Let's see, first he went by Self-Help for the Elderly." She turned to me, explaining, "That's one of the best social agencies in Chinatown. They kind of draw all the strings together, they know where to go to get help for all kinds of problems." She paused. "Jimmy and I are more of a shoestring operation—we try to help when it's something that local, state and federal funds won't cover. We aren't funded by any government programme. We have our hand out to take money from people and private groups." She turned back to Dan. "That couldn't be where he found . . . whatever it is. He was going to Self-Help to talk about Eddie Leong. Eddie ruptured a disc in his back, unloading crates of vegetables, and he doesn't know how to file for workman's comp. So, anyway, after Self-Help, Jimmy was going to Ping Yuen to see the Chan family and from there to a tenement on Stockton to talk to the Lees and try to find out more about Yuan."

She studied the sheet a moment longer, then said decisively, "That takes care of Wednesday. On Thursday, he put down the East Wind Restaurant, the Green Door Hotel and the Middle Kingdom Gallery." She squinted at the sheet. "By the hotel, he has the name E. Chow in parentheses."

Dan was writing down the names. "What's this Middle Kingdom Gallery? That doesn't ring any bells."

"It's fairly new, a high-class antique shop. The owner's Wilkie Lee."

I looked at Dan but his face didn't change at all. He saw my question and shook his head. "No relation. Lee's the most common name in Chinatown. There are lots of Lees, Wongs, Moys, Chans, etc. There are only about a hundred surnames in all of China and, since most American Chinese came from only a few districts around Canton, there are only about twelve or fourteen common last names here." He turned back to Lily. "I still don't place it. Where . . ."

"It's next door to Ted Moy's curio shop."

"Oh, sure," Dan said. "There used to be a bakery there."

Lily nodded. "But I'm sure Jimmy just went there to ask Wilkie for a donation."

Dan grinned. "Relax, Lily. Jimmy didn't rip anything off of the Gallery. It isn't that particular kind of treasure." He scrawled another note on his sheet. "Okay, so far as we know, on Wednesday and Thursday this is where Jimmy went—

66

Self-Help for the Elderly, Ping Yuen, the Lees', the East
Wind Restaurant, the Green Door Hotel and the Middle
Kingdom Gallery."

Six places where Jimmy Lee had walked on Wednesday
and Thursday, knocking on doors, smiling, entering. In one
of them had he come across the most famous fossils in the
world?

I was too old to believe in pots of gold or rainbows or maps
with X marking the spot. But I had seen and held that skull,
that distinctive unmistakable skull. Jimmy could have found
it anywhere in San Francisco. There was no guarantee that
we had traced all of Jimmy's activities on Wednesday and
Thursday.

But, we did know six places he had gone. Perhaps, at one
of them . . .

EIGHT

Even living on Russian Hill for six months hadn't trained me for the steep climb up Washington Street. The sidewalk angled sharply up and pedestrians bent like alpine hikers. We passed noodle cafes, apothecaries and tiny grocery stores. Orange crates balanced on boxes on the sidewalk and fresh produce beckoned shoppers. Dan pointed out twisted and brown arrow-root, taro, huge white radishes, winter squash and bok choy, Chinese cabbage. Squeezing past the crates, I smelled the cellar-like scent of earth and dampness.

Self-Help for the Elderly filled to bursting a string of tiny rooms that fronted onto Old Chinatown Lane, a narrow dead-end alley not far from Stockton. Every inch of space was utilized, workers squeezed behind desks stacked high with papers and folders. Phones rang, people came in and out and there was a constant hum of voices, speaking English and, Dan told me, Cantonese, its musical intonations rippling like water slipping over rocks.

It took a few minutes to find out who Jimmy had seen on Wednesday. We ended up in a narrow cubicle formed by a partition on one side and file cabinets on the other. Annie Jiu was on the telephone. She smiled and pointed to a couple of chairs. We slid sideways into them.

It came to me abruptly that she would be finished in a moment and would turn to us. What in the world were we going to say? We couldn't ask if she was the one who had Peking Man. If she did, she surely wouldn't admit it. If she didn't, we would almost be committed to long and difficult explanations. Worse than that, we didn't want to start the swirl of rumours that Peking Man was somewhere in China-town. That, at all costs, must be avoided.

I left it to Dan. When he spoke, I decided there were no flies on him.

"Annie, this Ellen Christie." We smiled at each other. "Dr Christie's visiting here from Arkansas, doing a special study on the role of social agencies in an urban society as opposed to a rural situation. She has a letter of introduction to Jimmy but he's out of town so I'm trying to shepherd her around. She's particularly interested in whether your problems in Chinatown are different or similar to those in her home area."

Annie didn't answer for a long moment. For that, I didn't blame her.

She looked at me curiously but answered very pleasantly. "Research for publication?"

I nodded and wished I could kick Dan. I cleared my throat. It was certainly time for me, the dauntless researcher, to offer something.

"It's a bit narrower than that," I improvised. "Of course, we do deal in different situations. Boone County is primarily agricultural so we have a good deal of seasonal labour. Straw-berries and peanuts. You know the problems there." I nodded sagely and she nodded in return. "I'm attempting," and I was amused at the suddenly pontifical depth to my voice, "to determine whether different qualities are needed by social workers in such disparate conditions. If you don't mind, I'd be interested in knowing something about you per-sonally and what qualities, in your view, are particularly helpful to work in Chinatown."

"Good Grief," Annie replied simply. She smiled a little. "I don't think it much matters whether you work in Chinatown or in the Bronx. It all comes down to people. People in trouble. People who need help." She stared thoughtfully at a bright red poster thumbtacked to a bulletin board. A full-jowled dragon tossed his head and thick black letters proclaimed the Chinese New Year celebration which would end with a huge parade on Saturday night. "Of course, Chinatown is a world all its own. There's no other like it. It's the largest Chinese community outside of Asia, almost fifty thousand Chinese in a twenty-four block area. But there's a lot more to make it unique than numbers. Historically, and that's still true today, it was the landing place for new immigrants. But, it's changed a lot. Do you know anything about what happened to the Chinese who came to America in the early days?"

I shook my head.

She said a little helplessly, "I scarcely know where to start, but you have to know the past to understand the present." She frowned, then began, "They came originally because there was no living to be had in China, no way, no hope for the future, nothing. Then came the gold strike in California and they immigrated by the thousands, coming to Gum Sahn, the Land of the Golden Mountains, as they called America. They worked in the mines, they cleared the swamps, laid the railroad tracks to the East, they did all the rough nasty jobs you couldn't hire anyone else to do and they did them without complaint because it was a living and a little over, enough to send money home to China to save their families. It was exciting then to come to America, a time of hope and promise. America liked the new immigrants, the sober, industrious, peaceable Chinese; liked them until times got bad and jobs were hard to find and, suddenly, the Chinese were an alien people, mentally and morally inferior, loathsome, dangerous. That was the start of almost seventy-five years of persecution by the government, Chinese immigration forbidden, the Chinese driven from jobs in all industries, relegated only to cooking and washing clothes and migrant labour, hounded out of towns up and down the West Coast; beaten, murdered, forbidden to become citizens, to marry whites, to own property. That's why Chinatown grew and prospered. There was no other safe place for most Chinese.

"During World War II, when Chinese Americans were recognized as citizens with the rights of citizens, Chinatown began to shrink and people talked of how it might dwindle to nothing because most American-born Chinese were growing up and leaving Chinatown. Their parents had been willing to make every sacrifice for their educations so they went to college and moved to the suburbs. They are artists, teachers, doctors, lawyers, restaurant owners, you name it. The home-grown Chinese are like any other second- and third-generation Americans. Their kids play Little League baseball, the girls are in ballet. I'd estimate there are about three hundred thousand Chinese in the United States today and most of them are like you and Dan, as American as popcorn and Coke.

"But that's not true in Chinatown for two distinct reasons that explain why there still is a Chinatown and why it is so different from your Boone County. Since the immigration reforms in 1965, more than 40,000 immigrant Chinese have settled in Chinatown. They arrive broke, bewildered and most of them not speaking a word of English. That's one unique fact. The other is the great number of old people in Chinatown. Out of a population of about fifty thousand, some ten thousand are old people. And nine out of ten of those old people are poor. Many of them are immigrants who squeaked into the U.S. in the 1920s and 30s with false papers. They came to work and send money back to China. The war and the Communist takeover stranded them here and now they are old and all alone.

"So, here in Chinatown today, you have people trying to make it in a foreign country and you have the old and lonely poor." She paused and spread her hands. "We don't run out of things to do," she said simply.

I felt suddenly ashamed of the role I was playing, pretending to be a social worker to someone who was spending her life helping others. It took a sharp nudge of Dan's foot to push me ahead.

"Are you a native of Chinatown? Is that how you became interested in social work?"

Annie smiled. "No. I'm from Peking and I . . ."

An electric shock couldn't have startled me more. I forgot all feelings of shame.

". . . never intended to stay in the United States. I came here in 1946 to study. I was sponsored by my mission school. I planned to go back to China and teach but I was stranded here by the Revolution." She paused and her gentle civilized face was thoughtful. "I don't know, perhaps I should have gone back, but you know the climate in China then, there wasn't any place for people like me. The churches were suspect and the church schools and that was my background. Sometimes I wonder . . ." She broke off, shook her head again. "You can't second-guess life. I've been happy here and especially since last year when my mother was able to come, oh, that's been so wonderful, to see her again, to hear of my brothers and their families . . ."

She came from Peking. Could she have brought Peking Man with her, years before? But why should she have hidden the fossils if she had them? Because of family still in China? But now, her mother here, could she have decided it might be safe to try and dispose of them through someone like Jimmy? Or, perhaps, had her mother brought them when she came to the United States?

Annie was still tracing her background. "Of course, I was lost for awhile when I decided it would be dangerous to try and go home to China. I taught for a year or so in Chicago, I waited tables in a restaurant in Albuquerque and finally ended up as a secretary in an import-export house in Los Angeles. But I was never satisfied, you know? Then I came up to San Francisco one weekend with friends and we visited in Chinatown and I saw all those old people, little old women in their shiny black slacks and narrow black slippers and shabby short coats—and I wondered how my mother was in Peking. You see, that was in 1972 and I had not heard from her, not a word, since 1947. So I came here and . . ."

The telephone rang. With a murmured apology, she broke off and picked up the receiver. We couldn't help overhearing.

"Yes, this is Annie . . . Oh, no . . . oh, Bobby, that's awful, awful . . . I meant to visit her yesterday, oh, I wish I had . . . yes, I'll come . . . no, there's no one to notify, she had no one . . . all right, Bobby."

No one has to say when news is bad. Her plump cheeks sagged and she suddenly looked middleaged. I knew, from her background, that she wasn't young. She had, until that telephone call, seemed young.

"She shouldn't have given up," Annie said and her voice was almost querulous. "It wasn't that bad. We would have helped. She shouldn't have given up."

"What happened, Annie?" Dan asked gently.

She lifted haunted dark eyes. "I did everything I could." Her mouth twisted and she turned to me. "You want to know a difference between Chinatown and your Boone County?" She didn't wait for a reply. "Until a few years ago, Chinatown had the highest suicide rate in the whole United States. That's something, isn't it? Then Self-Help for the Elderly got started in 1966. We made a difference. Old people knew somebody cared." She drew a deep breath. "There aren't as many suicides now, but there are still too many. So many."

She pulled out the bottom drawer of her desk, lifted out her handbag. "I'll have to go. There isn't anyone else." She closed the drawer with a sharp bang. "She was seventy-three and she had ninety dollars a month to live on. She just made it. You know the way, a cup of weak tea for breakfast, rice for lunch and the Self-Help for the Elderly evening meal for fifty cents at the school on Stockton. Fifty dollars a month for her room, that tiny box of a room at the Green Door Hotel. The big extra expense was her medicine, heart medicine, the little bottle of tablets cost $15. But she was making it."

Annie pushed back her straight chair, stood. "Last week the notice went up on the bulletin board at the Green Door. Somebody read it to her. The rent was going up five dollars a month. For her it might as well have been five hundred."

She snatched her raincoat from the wooden tree next to her desk then stopped and looked down at us forlornly. "I don't know why I'm in such a hurry now. It's too late now. Isn't it?"

Neither of us answered.

"If you want to see what it's like to be old and alone in Chinatown, you can come with me."

She was angry, too. Upset, angry, wanting to strike out, wanting most of all for someone to share the hurt with her, make it more bearable. And we were there.

I started to shake my head, that old instinctive reaction, wanting to evade the unpleasant, shrinking away from the role of spectator, the horrid image of the morbidly curious.

But Dan's hand was on my elbow. "All right, Annie. We'll

74

come. Maybe we can help."

Help? Or was he remembering that Jimmy Lee had been at the Green Door Hotel yesterday?

It was two blocks to the Green Door Hotel. We walked quickly. I was vividly aware of the street and the people and I noticed now how many of the people we passed were old. The day was growing warmer and the sidewalks were crowded with tourists, office workers out for an early inexpensive lunch, shoppers, a nun with a group of darting eager children and everywhere, walking slowly, stopping to gaze at pressed ducks hanging in market windows and trays of barbecued pork, carefully counting the cost of tangerines in crates along the wall, squinting at fruit and nut cakes in the bakery window, were the elderly, shabbily dressed in grays and blacks, sometimes in pairs, most often alone.

Coming down the street toward us, her faded brown coat a little too big for her, a woven mesh shopping bag clutched tightly in small worn hands, was another old lady. Our eyes met and, for an instant, we stared at one another. Her face was round and softly crumpled and the colour of faded parchment. She smiled suddenly, a gentle, trusting, open smile. I smiled in return and then she was past me and I wondered who she was and where she had come from and how her days had led her to Chinatown, to end her days in Chinatown.

We turned the corner, walked a block, turned another corner and Annie stopped at an unmarked door between a grocery and a browncurtained window.

You wouldn't find the Green Door Hotel unless you knew where it was or looked very hard. A faded sign, green letters edged in peeling gilt, hung crookedly just above the second story. A small grocery was to the right of the door. Dan told me later that the unmarked covered windows to the left masked a garment factory and, once inside, if you paused on the narrow uncarpeted stairs and listened, you would hear the whirr and thump of sewing machines and, softly, like the chirp of spring birds, women's voices, talking as they worked.

The air in the stairwell was damp and chill and smelled of cooking rice and mildew. Annie led the way, her shoes clicking loudly on the wooden steps. She paused at the top of the staircase.

"Bobby? Bobby?"

He was shuffling down the unlit hall toward us. The stair landing widened out just enough for a tiny reception area to the right. A battered card table and straight-backed chair served as the desk.

He called out to Annie in Chinese and she replied. I looked at Dan but his face was as blank as mine.

"I don't even speak enough Cantonese to get along," he said. "And they're speaking Mandarin."

I suppose he realized how little I knew about the Chinese language when I didn't answer.

"Mandarin's the official language, what most Chinese speak. But almost all American Chinese are from southern China, from only a few villages and districts around Canton, and they speak Cantonese. Annie is from Peking, the north, so she speaks Mandarin as do many of the refugees in the last ten years, especially those who were well-to-do landowners and fled the Communists because their lands were taken over."

He added a little grimly, "Those aren't the kind of immigrants you find in Chinatown."

Annie's voice rose in a question. Bobby shook his head.

Dan and I waited awkwardly, not belonging, intruders in a stranger's drama. Seventy-three, Annie had said. I wondered where in China seventy-three years ago a baby had cried. Had that baby girl been nestled in loving arms, wrapped gently in clean cloth, or had she been a burden, an extra mouth, out-cast from her beginning? Now that breath was stilled in an alien land in the chill of a lonely room.

The door banged downstairs and heavy footsteps clumped slowly up the wooden steps. Dan and I looked down and a prickle of distress moved down my back.

We moved aside, pressed against the wall, to let them pass, the two young ambulance attendants with the empty stretcher.

We heard them go on up the stairs, Bobby leading the way. And we heard the clump of their returning footsteps, the stretcher not empty now. But, when they passed us, a blanket spread the length of the stretcher, there was scarcely a hump beneath it. She must have been small, so small.

Annie watched until the stretcher was gone from sight, until the door banged in its frame downstairs. She closed her eyes briefly then turned to us. "This way," she said dully. "Upstairs."

Ru'lan Wong had lived on the top floor of the Green Door Hotel. If possible, it was even dingier than downstairs, the walls had been painted so long ago they were now just an in-determinate gray-brown. Some squares of the linoleum floor were missing and it gave the hall an odd hop-scotch appear-ance. It was very quiet. Faintly, I could hear mournful country western guitar. Nothing else.

"It's almost deserted this time of the morning," Annie said softly. "Most of them go out, go down to Portsmouth Square. They'll spend the day there, talking to their friends, sitting on the benches, watching the children, playing checkers and Chinese chess."

The door to Mrs Wong's room was ajar. We stopped at the threshold. Tiny, perhaps nine feet by twelve, it was cluttered but immaculate . . . except for the irregular puddle of blood that spread darkly across the neatly spread newspaper.

Annie stared down at the newspaper and I knew she was seeing a tiny old figure, kneeling, opening a paper, perhaps staring with unseeing eyes at the vertical lines of characters, then, quickly, or was it reluctantly, slowly, drawing the sharp blade across a wrinkled wrist.

I put my hand in Annie's arm.

"Ru'lan was always so neat, so clean . . ." Abruptly, Annie pulled away and bent to fold over the newspapers.

Such a small room. A single bed with a dark iron headstand, a worn orange afghan spread over the sheets. A small table holding a wind-up alarm clock, a cheap green glass vase with a single carnation, a box of Kleenex. A hotplate balanced on an orange crate in one corner. Bright red cotton trim had been tacked to the edges of three orange crates that sat along one wall. It was her larder, two boxes of Jello, a sack of rice, a sack of sugar, tea, three tangerines, salt, cellophane-wrapped dried apricots.

We helped Annie pack away the few dresses, take down the pictures from the walls, a calendar, two snapshots, a pennant from Disneyland.

"Someone will move in by this afternoon. There is always a waiting list."

I looked at the now bare walls, at the tiny cold cubicle, and wondered how this could be better housing for anyone?

The Green Door Hotel. I shook my head. I did feel sure of one thing now. Wherever Jimmy had found Peking Man, it couldn't have been here.

NINE

It isn't how long you know someone but the quality of the time you share. I had never, until this morning, seen Annie Jiu. I had never, until last night, seen Dan Lee. But, the three of us, after the Green Door, could never be strangers again. Dan and I helped Annie distribute the little pile of worldly goods to Ru'lan Wong's friends. The hotplate to Max Chang. His had burned out last week. The groceries to Ed Wu on the second floor. The snapshots to Miss Mary Huang.

It didn't take long.

Outside again, on the sidewalk, we all stood quietly for a moment, blinking in the bright sharp sunlight. San Francisco wore her siren suit this morning, the sky sharply blue, the sea-fresh air deceptively warm from the February sun. The hills rose behind us and fell away in front toward the Embarcadero.

Annie reached out, touched Dan's hand, then mine. "Thank you for coming with me. Thank you so much." She turned quickly away then and we watched her sturdy figure down the hill.

Dan's arm came around my shoulders and he gave me a brief hard squeeze, then his arm dropped away. "You're all right, Ellen."

I looked up at him and for that instant we saw into each other's eyes without presence or defence. I smiled a little. "You're all right, too."

He shrugged that away. But I knew now that Jimmy wasn't the only Lee with a kind heart.

79

We walked back to Grant, turned north. I hurried to keep up with Dan's long strides but, once again, I was looking at the people we passed, seeing more than camera-laden tourists. Mid-morning on a Friday and I was struck with how few families we passed. A few, of course. And some teenagers, laughing, jostling each other on the narrow sidewalk, cheerful, out, I realized suddenly, for a morning visit to Chinatown. Chinese, yes, but American Chinese, their patter the national language of youth with only that particular rising inflection at the end, that telltale 'Don't you think, huh?', to mark them as Californians. They would be as comfortable as sightseers in New Orleans or Philadelphia. They weren't Chinatown. No, Chinatown was the occasional prosperous businessman, the more harried less affluent small shopkeeper, the workers, office, store and manual, and, everywhere, walking slowly, bent and spare, the elderly.

This end of Grant, the north end, caters to Chinese shoppers, small groceries, laundries, sandwich shops, and, on the corner ahead, the Ping Yuen Bakery, named after the public housing units on Pacific.

At Pacific, as we waited for the light to change, Dan pointed ahead, "There's Ping Yuen. Jimmy's second stop on Wednesday."

It was public housing with a difference, lime green walls, bright red pillars and Chinese characters enscribed on the balconies.

"It looks nice."

"It's a damn sight better than the Green Door and other tenement hotels. Only one drawback."

"What?"

"It houses about 400 families but there are always about 2,000 on the waiting list. It takes about four years to get in."

"Is this the only public housing in Chinatown?"

"Yeah. For now. Construction's supposed to start pretty soon on some new. There'll be room for about 220 families and thousands have already signed up."

Ping Yuen had something else the Green Door lacked. Four little girls, their black hair neat and pretty in pigtails, played hopscotch, and their high happy voices followed us down the sidewalk.

As we pushed through the main doors, Dan looked back at the little girls. "It's an okay place for kids. Ping Yuen is the only public housing in the United States where more than ninety per cent of the kids who grow up in it go on to college."

Only in Chinatown, I thought.

We found the Chan apartment on the second floor toward the back. Dan had scarcely knocked when the door opened and a little boy about three poked a curious face around the edge, looked at us solemnly, then drew back his head before we could say anything.

We could hear the soft murmur of a radio, a girl laughing, the lilting sound of Cantonese, a rush of water.

Then the door swung wide. A plump sweet-faced woman looked at us shyly.

"Mrs Chan?" Dan asked.

She nodded.

"Is your husband home?"

She looked from Dan to me and back again and her dark eyes were uncertain.

"Could we talk to you for a moment?" Dan asked. "I'm Dan Lee, Jimmy Lee's brother, and . . ."

She held up her hands. *"Ngaw mm wuey gong ying mum,"* and turned away from the door. She called out to someone.

"She said she didn't speak English," Dan explained. "I know enough Cantonese for that."

The girl who came to the door smiled at us in a friendly

way. "Hi. Can I help you? I'm Mary Chan." Sleek dark hair framed a lovely heart-shaped face. She wore pale pink slacks and a white-and-pink patterned blouse.

Dan introduced us, then tried to explain why we had come. A new story this time.

"Ellen is new at Trouble, Inc, and she's following up on Jimmy's recent cases."

Mary nodded politely, but didn't say anything.

Dan paused, tried again.

"Jimmy came here Wednesday . . ."

She nodded, smiled again. "That is my father's day off so we asked Jimmy to eat with us."

Her mother stood close, looking at her, then at us. She asked Mary something in Cantonese and the girl replied then turned back to us.

"Please come in. We wish to welcome Jimmy's brother and fellow worker."

The living room was simply furnished, one sofa, two easy chairs, a straight chair. Dan and I sat on the sofa, Mrs Chan on a chair beside us and Mary in the straight chair.

I heard a soft giggle and looked down the narrow hall and saw the little boy who had come to the door and two girls about seven and eight. Mrs Chan saw me looking at them and called out and slowly, shyly, they came into the living room and crossed to their mother.

"My brother, Allen, and my sisters, Ruth and Lisa," Mary said.

There was an awkward silence.

Dan cleared his throat. "Actually, we're backtracking . . ." At Mary's quick frown, he rephrased it, ". . . introducing Ellen to the people Jimmy's helped. She's going to work with him. Now, if you could explain to us why Jimmy came to see you . . ."

Mary still looked puzzled.

"I mean, what is your difficulty? What help do you need?"

Mary spoke to her mother and Mrs Chan began to shake her head and words tumbled out. Mary nodded then laughed and looked at me. "It is all confusion, yes? We need nothing now. Jimmy, he has already helped us. It was to celebrate that we asked him to come on Wednesday."

When we sorted it all out, it was happiness that brought Jimmy to Ping Yuen. Not all of Chinatown was desperate or ill or old. Sometimes, yes, things went right and I was glad that good things were happening to the Chans, Mary told us, interrupted by short translations to her mother and rapid streams of Cantonese from Mrs Chan.

It was in October that her father had lost his job. He had been a dishwasher, earning $390 a month, working ten hours a day, six days a week. They had been living then in two un- heated rooms in a tenement on Stockton, her parents, Mary, the three younger children. There was one toilet on each floor, a kitchen serving two floors. People ate in shifts, bathed and washed in shifts.

Mary's voice dropped almost to a whisper. "It was bad, you know. I was frightened because . . . my father, one night he cried. There was no work, no job, no chance. He said . . ." she hesitated, then blurted out, ". . . he said America was a lie, a trap. There was no chance for him, nothing. And you see he had brought us, had come because he believed life would be better for us, that we would have a better chance, be able to go to school and that it didn't matter how bad it might be for him and my mother, it would be better for us." She took a deep breath. "But it wouldn't be better if we could not even eat. You see, in Hong Kong, he had a better job, he was foreman in a toy factory, but here, we came five years ago, he could not speak English and the only jobs he could get were in

Chinatown—dishwasher, janitor, waiter. It was hard to find any job and none of them paid enough but you could not complain because there were twenty people for every job and a man was lucky to get any work, no matter how little it paid. But then, you see, one night he was very tired and the water was too hot and his right hand was scalded, so he couldn't work, you see. So he was fired."

I interrupted sharply, "But that's outrageous! An employer owes a duty to his workers if there's an injury . . ." My words trailed away. Mary and Dan both shook their heads.

"No minimum wage. No unions. Not in Chinatown." Dan's voice wasn't angry or especially vehement or even bitter. It was resigned. "It's all hidden, of course. Jimmied time cards, no claims made."

"But, I don't understand how that can happen."

"Too many people, too few jobs. Thousands of new immigrants come every year and most of them are broke and, pretty soon, desperate for work. They can't speak English so they have to find a job in Chinatown. Every job, no matter how little it pays, has a line waiting for it."

He looked past Mary and her mother and the three little children; looked at the windows that glistened and sparkled in the sunshine, clean windows in an immaculate room. Poverty here, yes, but pride and hope, too.

Dan spoke softly now, to himself. "That's why I don't come to Chinatown. Almost never. I guess that's why I was mad at Jimmy. His being here, working here, reminded me of how tough and grim and frightening a place it really is.

"Yeah," and Dan's voice was suddenly angry, "the next time somebody raves about Chinatown's restaurants and says, 'It's such good food and CHEAP, too'," his voice rose in mimicry, "the next damn time, tell 'em why they're so cheap."

Mrs Chan frowned at Dan's angry tone, whispered to

Mary. Before Mary could finish her translation, Mrs Chan spoke and the words flew out in a furious rush.

Mary looked from her mother to Dan. "My mother say no, not to talk so, that it is not the fault of the restaurants, they must offer their food at less because there are so many, so very many places to eat, but, even so, everyone should be glad there are so many because it means many jobs, too. It is as a waiter that my father works now. Jimmy found the job for him. My father works hard, very hard, but it is a job, you understand, and, if a man can work, he can live, and here in this so great country my brother and sisters and I can go to school and grow up and have opportunities, many more than in Hong Kong and you should come to Chinatown to eat, come often, and not be unhappy that people work for so little but be happy that . . ."

"I know," Dan interrupted gently. "Tell your mother I understand. What she says, that is the Chinese litany."

"Litany?" Mary repeated. A faint blush spread in her cheeks. "I didn't know a word of English when we came five years ago. So there are some words, a lot of words . . ."

"A prayer," Dan explained. "A kind of prayer." He smiled. "My parents had faith, too, Mary. They grew up in Chinatown and they had a little grocery, the mom-and-pop kind of thing, a little grocery and six kids and all of those kids finished college . . . except one . . . and all of them left Chinatown and they have good lives, Mary, so tell your mother I believe, too. It's just . . . sometimes you hate to see people have to struggle so hard. But tell your mother, I understand."

Mrs Chan was smiling by the time Mary finished her translation. Smiling and nodding. Then, jumping to her feet and gesturing, she began to move toward the tiny kitchen.

We had tea then, pale green tea with a delicate flavour and Mrs Chan told us, through Mary, of their decision to come to the United States and the feeling of panic when they first arrived, Mary just a little girl and Ruthie a baby in arms, and walked away from the ship and they could not understand a word of English. The Chinese Newcomers' Service had helped them then. The good times and the bad and now—she spread open her arms—the wonderful space and happiness in Ping Yuen, Mary going to school a half-day, working a half-day, oh, everything was working out.

And nothing in any of her recital seemed remotely connected to Peking Man.

"Did you and Mr Chan come from Peking?" I asked.

But Dan was shaking his head. Later, he explained that all Cantonese-speaking Chinese are from southern China.

Mary told us that her mother's family had lived at Toishan, a village not far from Canton until after World War II, leaving for Hong Kong just before the Communist victory in the Civil War. Mr Chan's family had fled from Luchow to Hong Kong in 1947 when Mr Chan was ten. He and Mrs Chan had met in Hong Kong.

"Do you keep in touch with your families?"

Mrs Chan had shrugged. For so many years, it had not been possible to communicate with the mainland. She had heard recently from a Hong Kong cousin who had visited Canton. This cousin wrote that things were better, so much better than they had been before in China. Mrs Chan broke off, hesitated, than Mary translated her hasty addition. "But not, of course, as good as things in the United States."

I understood that swift addition. The fear of offending, of saying the wrong thing, that was the great gulf between Mrs Chan and someone like Dan or me, American-born, sure of our place. Could he and I ever quite understand an immigrant's uncertainty?

And could we ever be quite sure of our perceptions?

Walking down Pacific, turning back onto Grant, we agreed the Chans certainly didn't seem likely to have Peking Man. Would they even have any inkling of such fossils' worth?

But lack of facility in English doesn't mean someone is stupid. And we had no way of knowing where Mr and Mrs Chan's fathers had been during World War II. Had either perhaps served with the northern guerillas who harassed the Japanese and fought so many battles not far from Peking?

We could be sure of one thing only. The Chans had especially invited Jimmy to their apartment on Wednesday. Jimmy was their friend. They would trust him.

TEN

The Chans were making it. Just barely, perhaps. Poor as government figures count poverty, but, in their own judgment, making it; secure in a bare but comfortable apartment, earning enough to eat tolerably, the children in school.

Yuan Lee's family wasn't making it.

I wondered, as we climbed the narrow dirty stairs of the tenement, why it was so cold and dank in a tenement. My own apartment was unheated. I did have a little electric heater to chase away the early morning chill, but it was never this cold in the stairwell of my apartment house, not even on the chilliest and foggiest July night.

Despair is the death of hope, an old emotion, a cold emotion. This building stank of urine and dirt and despair. It was as palpable as the stickiness of the stair rail, the squashed cups and cans underfoot.

The metal number, 3, on the Lees' door hung by only one nail, had slipped down to dangle, an odd metal curlycue, upside down, meaningless.

Dan knocked and the sound was loud in the sombre quiet of the narrow hallway.

The door opened slowly. The light in the hall was so dim that it took a moment to see her in the doorway, young and thin, dressed in a too-tight red blouse and dirty gray slacks. From behind her, somewhere in the dimness of a small cramped room, came a low cry, a moan of anguish.

There was such a wave of sorrow and pain spreading out from that shadowy room that I knew, for an instant made my own, the grief and horror that must have swept Pandora when she lifted that lid on darkness.

The girl in the doorway, near in age to Mary Chan, stared wordlessly at us. Mary had smiled, her mouth curving in welcome. This girl's face was rigid, her lips clamped tightly shut.

"We came about Yuan," Dan began, then his confident voice fell away as the girl pressed the back of a balled fist against that rigid mouth. She stared at us with huge dark strained eyes.

"About Yuan?" Her voice was thin, almost expressionless. Her mouth stretched in a travesty of a smile. "Oh, that's good of you." Her words minced now, mocking the empty meaningless phrases of a world that does not really give a damn. "Are you from welfare? Or the truancy office? Or . . ." She began to laugh, a high shrill angry laugh. "You're too late. Did you know that? Too damn late. You wouldn't help him when he needed it. No. What difference did it make what happened to one more lousy no-good Chink street kid? You didn't care."

Tears furrowed down through too-thick makeup. Hands still closed in tight angry fists, she rubbed at her eyes.

I reached out, touched her arm. "Please, tell us . . ."

"Oh, Yuan, Yuan," and she cried, great wrenching sobs that shook her frail shoulders. In gasps and broken phrases, she grieved for her brother. ". . . never had a chance . . . never . . . the kids laughed at him, laughed at the way he talked so he quit school . . . lousy jobs . . . sweeping up in a fish market but no chance to do better . . . no money . . . and he never could get English, couldn't get it . . . oh, Yuan . . . he was mad at me because I learned . . . yeah, I could speak it and once he cried because he couldn't say it, couldn't . . ."

She quieted finally, leaned against the dirty cracked plaster wall, rested and caught her breath. She didn't look at us. She looked down a grimy hall at darkness.

When she did look at us, there was fear in her eyes. "You know about the gangs?" It was almost a whisper.

I looked at Dan, who nodded, so I said nothing.

"Guys over here from Hong Kong, out on the streets," she said tiredly. "But Yuan wasn't like that, not really. It was just that there wasn't any place for Yuan, no place to go but nothing to come home to. See, he quit school and the rest of us," she tossed her head toward the room behind her, "we were all in school and Momma at the garment factory and Daddy at the fish market. And, at nights, when everybody was home, well, there isn't any room and everybody's tired . . . and kinda hungry . . . so Yuan started hanging out with these guys."

She looked uneasily up and down the hall, leaned closer to us, whispered. "It's dangerous, see, to know too much about the gangs. They get guys who don't pay when they gamble, they make sure everybody pays up. They sell . . . they sell anything you want. And they fight. Somebody steals somebody's girl, something like that."

She had begged Yuan to stay out of the streets.

"He got a job last week." She said it proudly, almost forgetting for a moment. Then her face crumpled again, a woman's face behind a child's. "He was going to be all right. I was going to help him with his English." Tears still glistened on her face but her eyes were dark and empty when she looked up at us. "It doesn't make any difference now that he couldn't speak English. It doesn't matter at all."

"I'm sorry," I said helplessly, "so sorry."

But that didn't make any difference either. That I was sorry. Or not sorry. No difference to Yuan Lee.

"He was just going out for a little while Tuesday night. Just because he'd promised some guys. But he wasn't going to stay with them. It was Momma's birthday and he was going to get home by the time she got off work. He promised."

She looked at me. "Yuan always did what he promised," she said simply. "So when he didn't come . . . I think I knew then. That's why I called the police Wednesday." She was bitter now. "They didn't care. So what's new? Some Chink kid, a gang kid, doesn't come home. So what?"

Tears edged from the corners of her eyes again. "They don't know who killed him. Somebody from the Jade Dragon gang, the policeman said. He said it was just another gangfight. He said . . ." her young mouth quivered and we had to lean close to hear the pain-filled words, ". . . people get what they deserve."

Yuan Lee died at nineteen. Of massive haemorrhaging. Three stab wounds in his back. One had punctured his heart. He had been stuffed into a black plastic lawn bag and hidden in the deep shadows behind one of the massive fir trees in the square across from the Old St Mary's Church. Not far from the stainless steel statue of Sun Yat-sen. It was a church caretaker who noticed the awkwardly-shaped bundle where no bundle should have been.

Yuan must have died Tuesday night. He wasn't found until late Thursday afternoon.

That couldn't matter to Yuan Lee now, either.

Dan asked how we could help. Was the funeral planned? Was there anything we could do?

She shook her head. Her father was gone now to see about the funeral. He had taken the day off from work.

There was nothing we could do. Nothing anyone could do. Dan took out his billfold, pulled out a twenty and a five. She stepped back, shaking her head again, but he tucked the bills in her hand.

"I'm Dan Lee, Jimmy Lee's brother. This is from Jimmy. He wants you to have it."

We left her then, standing in that dingy narrow hallway, the bills crumpled in her hand, her face heavy with pain.

We were almost back to Grant Avenue, on our way to the East Wind Restaurant, before I could manage a word. And then it was just a bleat. "I don't see how Jimmy stands it!"

Dan didn't answer immediately. We skirted our way around crates of produce being unloaded on the sidewalk, squeezed by a knot of shoppers fingering vegetables in an outside display, then brought up at a red light.

"We grew up going to old St Mary's," Dan said quietly. "We were all altar boys." The light changed. He took my elbow. "This way," he directed and we walked down the hill.

"Jimmy was always . . . well, he listened better, I guess. You know that passage in the Bible, the one about, 'I was hungry and you fed me, sick and you ministered unto me, in prison and you visited me'?"

I nodded.

"You remember Jesus' listeners were puzzled and asked when had they done these things and Jesus explained . . ."

I finished it for him, " 'Inasmuch as ye have done it unto one of the least of these my brethren, ye have done it unto me'."

"Yeah. Well, Jimmy listened a little harder than some of the rest of us."

We were passing a meat market now. Barbecued chickens and Peking ducks hung by their necks in the window, fresh, plump, succulent. A well-dressed thirtyish woman stood by the counter, pointing at one duck, another, and the rings on her fingers shone in the bright overhead lighting. A suburban Chinese housewife shopping for the weekend, plump, prosperous, cheerful.

Dan paused to wave at the stooped old man behind the cash register.

As we walked on, he told me, "That's Tom Fong. He and his oldest son, Al, run the market. Al and I played basketball together at the Y, worked in our folks' shops after school. That's how almost everybody I knew grew up, working, living in a couple of rooms above the shop. That's the way it was in the forties and fifties; little stores, big families, everybody working. We were all poor, if you want to count the money, but we were together. That was when everybody marvelled at the Chinese family, at the total lack of juvenile delinquency among Chinese." He laughed and, for the first time in hours, I heard that infectious rollicking laughter that I knew instinctively was so much a part of him, the way he looked at life, laughed at it. "Whites believe the damndest things about Chinese—we never smile, we never cry, we're wily, devious, untrustworthy, we're always honourable, we nod and bow when we say hello, our kids never get in trouble, we gamble in smoke-filled opium dens."

"I did think," I said in a small voice, "that I'd read somewhere that Chinese teenagers were almost never in trouble."

"You read it," he agreed. "You read it and it used to be true. That was when families worked together and lived together. Mom worked, all right, from early morning until after dark, but it was right there in the store and the six of us were always with Mom or Dad. Those were the days that when your parents told you to smile, you smiled. If they told you to shut up, you shut up. Same thing at school. And every day, a thousand times, they told us that all we had to do was go to school and work hard and everything was possible."

We stopped for a red light. "I guess," and his voice was soft now, the laughter gone, "they weren't wrong, huh? I'm a lawyer, Pete's an engineer, Janet's a teacher, Eddie's a medical technician, Ruth's a pharmacist." He shook his head.

"Jimmy was working on a degree in Asian studies. But no matter how you cut it, it was mostly okay because Mom and Dad were there, we had each other, all the damn time. These kids today, hell, they come over here, most of them from Hong Kong, they can't speak English and suddenly everything's tough, but, worse than that, nobody's home to care or to help. The dad works eight, ten hours a day unloading vegetables, sweeping out a fish market, the mother's gone all day to the garment factory, home maybe to cook lunch and dinner. And what's home? A stinking crowded tenement, a john a floor, quarrels over who can use the kitchen when—everything goes sour, the family, then the kid."

He glanced sideways at me. "I don't believe in mothers working outside the home."

I didn't bristle, which surprised me a little. Instead, I thought for a moment then asked slyly, "Do your sisters work?"

For a moment his face was immobile then a tiny smile touched his lips. "Touché. Ruth and her husband, Ted, have a drug store in Richmond and Janet teaches."

"And their kids are okay?"

He was looking across the street. "There's the East Wind. Upstairs, just past the bank."

"Janet's and Ruth's kids?"

"Janet's Eddie has a four-year scholarship to Yale and her daughter, Pam, is a nurse. Ruth's Bobby is an Eagle Scout, Millie's in the high school choir, Bill makes straight A's." His mouth spread. "They have a little trouble with one of them."

"Oh?"

"Yeah, Ruth called me the other night, wanted me to come out and have a talk with Danny."

"Danny? Your namesake?"

94

He nodded. "Ruth said that was her first mistake. Well, if not the first, then . . . Anyway, Danny played hooky from Chinese school twice last week."

"Chinese school?"

"Oh, I forgot for a minute." He had forgotten that I was new to Chinese and Chinatown—and I was absurdly pleased. "Chinese school is the little extra, like two hours every evening, that Chinese kids go to after regular school. They study Cantonese, Chinese history, calligraphy. It's tough, tough stuff to study and tough to sit inside and work when your bottom aches from being behind a desk all day already. And, you see, a couple of weeks ago, I was out to Ruthie's for dinner and I got started on how I had hated Chinese school when I was kid and how lousy I did. And how I would cut out in the spring for baseball. Danny, of course, was drinking in every word. When they caught up with him, he said it was just what Uncle Dan had done!"

We waited for a car to pass then cut across Grant. A silken golden flag rippled from the second floor front of the East Wind Restaurant. Bright red wooden shutters masked the windows. Dragons curved and curled around the sign, EAST WIND.

Dan held the door for me and we started up thickly carpeted steps. Satin wallpaper glistened golden and green and the air smelled faintly of sandalwood and cedar.

"Will you talk to Danny?" I asked.

We were midway up the steps. He paused for an instant, nodded slowly. "Oh sure. And I'll tell him how well his mom did in Chinese school and how his Uncle Pete won the award as the most outstanding student the year he was graduated— and how Uncle Dan wishes he had done better so that he could speak Cantonese." Dan smiled and it was almost wistful. "I remember how I hated it—but I'm damn glad I went, that they made me go."

"Why?"

"Because you have to know where you came from to know who you are."

ELEVEN

Opulent, elegant, magnificent, the East Wind Restaurant was more than just two blocks from the Lees' tenement. It was a world away. I just glimpsed the main dining room as Dan shook his head at the maitre d' and opened an inconspicuous door to the right of the stairs.

Green ferns glistened with drops of water in graceful hanging baskets. The rich ruby red of the carpet contrasted vividly with the sandalwood and gold of the walls. And the tables were spaced well apart, their damask cloths shiningly fresh and crisp.

It was early yet for the luncheon hour so only a few diners were scattered about. But I saw enough to know that even when every table was taken there would be an illusion of space and privacy.

Then the door closed behind us and we walked a few steps down a plain linoleum-floored hallway. Dan knocked at a second door.

"Come in."

The man behind the desk was writing as we opened the door. The desk sat sideways to the door, facing a glass wall that looked out into the restaurant proper and I knew the other side would appear to be a mirror. He continued writing for a moment. He was about Dan's age. His face, rounded and plump, looked heavy in repose, almost stolid. But, when he looked up, saw us, his face shifted, reformed into ebullience. Pushing back his chair, he jumped to his feet and moved toward us, hand outstretched.

I felt my own face reshaping, my mouth curving into a smile, and I marvelled at the impact of personality. This man possessed star quality, that indefinable elusive magnetism that exerts as automatic a pull as the moon on tides.

"Hey Dan, you good son-of-a-bitch, where've you been! Did Jimmy tell you I said you'd damn well better come by! What kind of miracle does it take to pull you back to Chinatown for a spell? And what kind of beautiful woman are you lucky enough to bring with you? I haven't seen such gorgeous eyes since Joanne Woodward ate here two years ago! By God, it's about time . . ."

Words swirled around us, glittering like brightly patterned butterflies, catching and reflecting for an instant his vitality.

Dan grinned, shook his hand, introduced us.

As we settled into the narrow couch beside his desk, Dan said, "Ellen, this is my youth making all these loud noises at you. You'd never believe Buddy was once the fastest kid in the fifth grade." Dan paused. "I mean the fastest kid around bases—although he's always had a quick mouth, too."

Buddy was at it again the minute Dan finished. "Don't let him kid you, Miss Christie . . ."

"Ellen," I interrupted.

He winked at me and it was as friendly and genuine as a pat on the arm. "Right on, Ellen. I'll have to set you straight about Dan. He hasn't always been an outstanding, trustworthy, sober, industrious light of the Bar. Why, I remember . . ."

And he reeled into a fantastic anecdote about the time Alan Ladd was making a movie in Chinatown (it was supposed to be Hong Kong, WWII) and Dan and Buddy were in high school and they hired on as extras, and Dan kept saying the stuntman's big scene was dead easy (it started on a four-

story rooftop, the stunt man running along an eight-inch parapet to the corner of the building, hunched over as Japanese
soldiers shot at him, then shinnying down a drain pipe to the
second story, lunging four feet in mid-air to catch onto the
fire escape platform, swinging hand over hand to the ladder,
jumping two steps at a time down the ladder, and, at the first
floor, dropping down to the alley).

Buddy dared Dan to try it and offered him twenty-five dollars.

"Okay, Ellen, think about it. Twenty-five bucks. Do you
have any idea how much money that was in 1956?" Buddy demanded. He studied me for a minute. "Nope. You must have
been pricing comic books about then. Anyway, there I was,
committed to paying this dumb jerk twenty-five bucks if he
made it to the alley. Of course, Dan fastened onto it like
Tarzan to Jane. Then I began to get bad thoughts. Like what
his family was going to do to me if he broke his fool neck. And
my family. And his girl friend, Micki Wong," this last with a
sly wink. "And the movie director if we messed up the alley
with a big splotch of blood. Most of all, worst thought in the
bag, where in hell was I going to get twenty-five bucks if he
didn't break his neck!"

"So Buddy began his career as an entrepreneur," Dan
laughed. "I've always been glad that I gave him his start."

I looked at Dan. "You didn't do it!" But I suppose I must
have known the answer before I asked.

"Oh hell yes," he answered, "but the winner and champion was Buddy. See, we had it planned for just after dawn
because that's when the movie company shot their scenes but
they were off that day, some kind of holiday. I got up there
and started and never knew 'til I made it to the alley, and
broke my damn ankle in that last piffling jump, that Buddy
had sold seats to everybody at school, renting the roof across

the street. Nobody made a peep until I was all the way down and landing in the alley. So I got paid my twenty-five bucks, all right. But Buddy had the last laugh. He cleared a cool fifty for himself, even after paying for the roof." Dan laughed again, then nodded toward the one-way mirror and the clear bright view of the elegant dining room, "Buddy took his fifty and ran with it—all the way to the top."

Buddy, too, looked out into the dining room and there was pride in his face, but awe, too, and a hint of disbelief. "I've been damn lucky, huh?"

"You've worked damn hard," Dan added.

"It takes more than work." Buddy shook his head slowly from side to side. "More than work." Then, lightly, he asked, "And how's the legal business. You come by to see me for fun or you looking for a client?"

"Now, Buddy, you know lawyers don't hustle like that. Much. No, I came to see you because of Jimmy."

Buddy was pleased. "I told him to tell you . . ."

"I haven't seen him. I'm hunting for him."

Dan didn't tell Buddy about Peking Man. But he told him the rest of it. I wondered how wise it was. But this was Dan's friend.

"A treasure?" he asked once, eyebrows lifting.

When Dan had finished, Buddy was shaking his head.

"No help here, Dan. Jimmy came to see me, yeah. A couple of things. Checking on jobs. I try to keep him in mind when a job opens up, dishwasher, salad bar, bus boy. But mostly he wanted to talk to me, see if I could get the Six Companies to back some kind of youth club, you know, a place for kids to come in off the street, maybe play a little pool, practice kung fu, maybe paint, make pottery. We've talked about it before. But, it isn't easy." Buddy's big shoulders drooped a little. "Everybody's always blaming the Six Companies for not doing this, not doing that. Hell, Dan, there just isn't that much money! Some of these kids think Six Companies is rolling but that's not true. We have an annual fund drive, you know, to raise money for the hospital and the Chinese school, and that takes almost every penny we can get together. And this other," Buddy shrugged, "it's hard to get older people to do anything for kids anymore."

Dan nodded. Turning to me, he said, "Buddy's on the board of the Six Companies." He paused. "That's a little hard to explain to an outsider, but the Six Companies is the main group in Chinatown that represents everybody . . . or tries to. A long time ago, when Chinese first came here, settled, they were lonely, far from home and the village associations that they had belonged to, so they formed groups here, like if you go to London and you join an Arkansas Club, say I'd join a California Club. Most Chinese here came from about eight of the ninety districts that make up the province of Canton. When they got here, the ones from the same district banded together and that's how you got the district associations. Also, they formed family name groups, like the Scottish clans. So you have the Lee Family Association, the Wong Family Association, etc. A lot of these groups argued about how things should be run in Chinatown and, finally, in the 1860s, each district association elected representatives to form the Six Companies. Ever since, the Six Companies has just about run Chinatown. And that's why Jimmy comes to see Buddy when he wants to get something done."

"I wish it were that easy," Buddy groaned.

Dan smiled briefly. "Nothing's ever easy. Especially not when you try to change things. Is that all Jimmy wanted?"

"Yes."

Dan sighed. "I don't know. Maybe we're going after it all wrong. We've seen almost everybody Jimmy talked to on

Wednesday and Thursday and we still don't have any idea where he found . . ."

I held my breath.

". . . the treasure."

I breathed again.

"Was he excited, Buddy? Any different from usual?"

Buddy frowned. He looked, his heavy face furrowed in thought, quite formidable.

Slowly, he shook his head.

We turned down Buddy's invitation to lunch. Dan promised, as we left, "I'll bring her back, Buddy. For a special dinner."

Buddy walked to the door with us. "The whole family, maybe?"

Dan had a curious expression on his face when he answered. "I think so, Buddy, yes."

I wondered, all the way down the red carpeted stairs and out into the rush and swirl of Grant Avenue, what that particular look meant. Was it embarrassment or pride or . . . But he didn't give me a chance to ask and his next words drove the question from my mind.

"Here we are," he said, "the Middle Kingdom Gallery, Jimmy's last stop."

It was the alcove just past the door that opened onto the steps leading up to the East Wind Restaurant. Just stepping into the alcove, I realised that this shop was different from many of the curio stores up and down the Avenue.

Dan saw my face as I looked through the plate glass at the display.

"Right. It's not the usual ticky tacky souvenir shop. See that chest." It was about three feet tall, classically simple in design, its wood the rich purplish red of rosewood. "That's a Ming chest. If it's authentic, it's worth a bundle—but even if

102

it's a copy from Hong Kong, it's still in the caviar class."

One vase sat alone in the other display window. It was bottle shaped with a plump base and a slender ridged neck. Its colours were rose and green softly swirled and misty smudges of pale cream. A typewritten card announced simply: MING THREE-COLOUR ENAMELWARE.

Dan was reaching for the door handle. "Since trade re-opened with China, several new stores have begun. They carry really nice stuff; porcelains, ivories, jade, lacquer-ware."

"So Jimmy went from a luxury restaurant to a luxury shop." My comment was an idle one but it had an unexpected effect.

Dan stopped, frowned, then rustled in his pocket for the list of Jimmy's visits. He stared at it for a long moment, then said, "That's funny."

"What's funny?"

He still stared at the list. "I'm sure I copied it correctly."

I waited patiently.

"That's damn funny. Why would Jimmy leave the East Wind Restaurant, go to the Green Door Hotel, then come here?"

"Why not?"

"Because it's roundabout. Look, the East Wind is right upstairs. Why didn't he drop in here, then go to the Green Door? Why go all the way to the Green Door, it's at least three blocks, then come back here?"

I had not remembered the order of Jimmy's visits on Thursday. I had followed Dan from place to place without question. But it was, I felt, important to retrace Jimmy's route. If he had gone first to the Green Door then so should we.

I caught Dan's hand as he began to open the door.

"Let's go to the hotel first."

"Why? Three blocks there, three blocks back, let's save our feet."

It is the instinct of an anthropologist to be tidy. If you set up certain criteria to check in the study of a population, skin colour, blood pressure, blood groups, basal metabolism, body size, composition, dental pattern, then, by God, you check that criteria on each subject.

If Jimmy had visited six places in a certain order, then we should visit those six places in the very same order.

I am, then, tidy. And determined.

The Green Door Hotel was as dingy, sombre and cheerless in the afternoon as in the morning. No sunlight penetrated the narrow hallway. We stopped at the battered card table. The straight chair was pushed under it. A crumpled newspaper lay on it and an empty pop bottle.

Dan walked on down the hall to the door with the manager's sign. He rapped sharply.

The sound echoed down the narrow hallway.

We waited. No one stirred beyond the door. No one came.

Dan looked at me as if to say, well, all right, here we are, what now?

I stepped up beside him, began to knock. And knocked and knocked.

A door behind us creaked open and a hoarse smoke-roughened voice demanded, "What the hell! What the hell! A man can't even rest in his own room—and you can pound from here 'til the cows come home and that damn Bobby won't answer you. Not today he won't!"

We had turned now to face the belligerent unsteady figure across the hall. A weathered work-callused hand gripped the door frame but, even so, he teetered a little and the smell of cheap red wine spread slowly in the airless hall. He had been a big man but age and ill-health had bent him like a wind-whipped tree. And he was the first man I'd seen in Chinatown with the stubble of a beard. His face sagged, deep lines furrowed his forehead and cheeks, and his eyes were watery and weak—and suspicious.

"Goddam Bobby." Then he shook his head. "Not his fault, though, not his fault." He leaned a little out into the hall, peering at us. "You part of it? You the goddam realtors?"

Dan shook his head. "What's wrong? Where's Bobby? Why won't he come to the door?"

"Too goddammed chicken, that's why. He put the notice under the doors yesterday, see. Five dollars more a month. But that's not the half of it—and he knows it."

"What's the rest of it?" I asked.

He looked at me then, fastened dark bleary eyes on my face, and I was shocked at the pain and despair and fear in those drugged eyes. Not enough wine to take the pain away. Maybe all the wine in the world couldn't take the pain away. His mouth quivered and I knew that he couldn't speak, couldn't bring himself to tell us.

I reached out, gently touched that gnarled hand gripping the door frame so tightly. His eyes followed my hand then swung back to my face. He blinked, moved his lips, then said so softly we scarcely could hear, "They're going to sell the building."

"Oh," Dan said and there was a world of understanding and sympathy in his voice.

The old man's mouth turned down in a bitter smile. "Yeah, they're going to pull it down and build a garage. You know how short parking is this close to the financial district." We could hear the parody in his voice—and the fear. He stared at us, his weak old eyes flickering from one to the other. "Where will we go?" he whispered. "Where will we all go?"

All the old people who clung to life in this dingy unheated tenement hotel would be forced out of their home, their only home. Here they could, just barely, eke out an existence, pay the rent, cook rice and salt pork, eat at Self-Help for the Elderly.

Where would they go?

"Are you sure it's true?" I asked.

The old man nodded hopelessly. "Bobby knows because of the insurance, not getting it renewed for another year. They're raising the rent to screw every last penny out of us for a couple more months, then wham, out we go. Bobby knows it's true and so he won't come to the door, he doesn't want to look at us and say it's true."

No, I wouldn't want to answer the door, either. Who would want to look into old, frightened eyes and say, oh yes, that's right, your world's ending, there isn't any place for you, it's the street for you, gather up your little boxes, your bags of rice and sugar, pick everything up and go, there's no place for you.

He drew himself up, raised his head and I could see the remnants of the man he once had been, a man with dignity and pride. "But that's not why you knocked for Bobby. It's nothing to do with you." He wavered in the doorway. "Can I help you?"

"We're looking for a friend . . . of a friend," Dan said. "E. Chow. Do you know, would you know who that is?"

The old man nodded gravely. "I'm happy to help you." He nodded again and I smelled sour red wine and wondered how much of it he had drunk this beautiful San Francisco morning. "The top floor. Room 42."

Dan smiled, a gentle warming smile and I liked Dan very much indeed. "Thank you. That's a real help." Dan reached for his wallet.

The old man started to shake his head. He wanted to shake his head. He remembered, he felt for a few minutes there the way he had felt years ago when he dealt with others, one man talking to another, helped people without a price.

But he needed that money.

It was a long time ago that he had stood straight.

He took the bill, curled it in his hand, mumbled a thanks and sank back into his room, almost slamming the door in his hurry.

Dan took my arm and we turned toward the stairs and I wondered what we would find.

E. Chow. Room 42.

TWELVE

Another shoe box of a room, nine feet across, twelve feet deep. An interior room, windowless, but, nonetheless, sparkling clean and cheerful with an inexpensive fern flourishing in a corner and orange-crate cabinets covered in brightly-coloured shelf paper.

She smiled and nodded and fussed about the tiny room, insisting that Dan take the only chair and shyly sharing the edge of the narrow bed with me.

"I'm so pleased to meet you, Mr Lee, and you, Dr Christie. Did Jimmy send you to visit me?" Her English was faintly British in accent, her voice soft and gentle.

"Not exactly, Miss Chow," Dan replied. "We are doing a follow-up on Jimmy's caseload and we wanted to check with all of his clients. Could you describe for us briefly what Jimmy was doing for you?"

She nodded slowly. On the door to her room a small white card was taped. It bore the name EMILY CHOW in an old-fashioned curling script. She matched that script, her white hair thick and soft, her black dress ankle-length and I guessed that she bought it at least thirty years ago. She wore a cameo brooch at the neck of her black dress, pinning a pale cream scarf. One hand lifted, touched that cameo, then dropped back to her lap. She clasped her hands, clasped them so tightly her hands were rigid.

Surprised, I raised my eyes to her face. She sat in profile to me on the bed. The smile had slipped away and her face was smooth, impassive.

She nodded again. "I first met Jimmy several months ago,

Mr Lee. I work as a volunteer at the Chinese Hospital. You know, visiting patients, taking books and puzzles around. Jimmy had come to visit Mr Wong who used to live down the hall here at the Green Door. Mr Wong was dying of cancer. I thought it very kind of Jimmy to come and visit an old man who was all alone and dying. I decided, Mr Lee, that Jimmy had a good heart."

It was very quiet in that small cheerful room. She reached down at the foot of the narrow bed and picked up her knitting, soft and fluffy, pink and pale yellow. She began to knit, the needles flashing, clicking softly.

"I felt in need of someone with a good heart this past week. So I called and asked Jimmy to come and see me." She looked up from her knitting and her brown eyes measured Dan. "I received word from China that my benefactor had died." She paused. "Did Jimmy tell you of this?"

Dan shook his head.

Her eyes fell away from his face. She looked down at the fluffy mass of wool, seemed almost to speak to herself.

"It was all so long ago now, so far away. The years pass so quickly, like petals drifting down, dropping so softly you scarcely realize they are gone until the stem is bare. Soon now . . ."

She did not finish. She was old and she looked ahead. Then, like a grizzled terrier, she shook herself a little, said briskly, "Mr Lee, I don't know how it can be of interest to you, but I will explain why I asked Jimmy to come. If you wish to know?"

We had come here, thrust ourselves upon her. It was clear that she couldn't be part of Jimmy fleeing down a Chinatown alley, a Peking Man skull in his gym bag. But simple courtesy required us to listen to the problem that she felt must be shared with someone of good heart.

Dan, I was sure, beneath his smooth impassive lawyer's face, would have liked to strangle me. It was my insistence that had brought us back to the Green Door. Later, he would likely have something to say about stubborn women, but, here and now, he smiled at her, "Yes, Miss Chow, we'd like to hear."

It was a story of duty, duty fulfilled, duty remembered. A story that could only have come out of China.

Her gentle cultivated voice carried us far from the Green Door, over an ocean, deep into a history that wasn't ours, that Dan, perhaps, from hearing older family members speak, might have some understanding of. To me, it was new, bizarre, compelling.

She wasn't sure how old she was, not within a year or so, for she had been cast off, abandoned by her family.

"It was not unusual, you see, for girl babies. They were unimportant. Another mouth to feed when the rains hadn't come and the crop sparse and most of it due the landlord. Many girl children could not be cared for and they were sold into slavery or prostitution. I always felt my family loved me for they left me, you see, at a Presbyterian mission. That's where I grew up, not too far from Peking, and it was from Mrs Macdonald that I learned English." Miss Chow smiled and her smooth ivory-toned face crinkled into happiness. "English and needlework and cooking—and oh so many hymns. We sang as we worked. It was a happy place to grow up."

But personal happiness in China was always as fragile and unaccustomed as prosperity—and never long-lived.

Famine and war washed over the mission. Times were hard and money from Scotland irregular and often long delayed.

"When I was sixteen, as we counted my birthdays, I knew I couldn't stay. The Macdonalds had taken in so many castaway girls. It was time for me to provide for myself. I told Mrs Macdonald I wanted to go out into the world."

Even now, all these long years later, I could hear the sorrow in her voice. Emily Chow had learned about duty, accepted duty early on.

All the skills she had mastered at the mission were useless in the eyes of most Chinese. Who would want as a wife a girl who had grown up with foreign devils and who spoke their language!

But Mr Macdonald returned from a journey to Peking, three days' walk with word of a home for Emily. She would live in the home of Dr Tang, a widower, and teach English to his children, rather like a British nanny. Dr Tang, most unusual for a Chinese in the 1930s, had travelled much abroad and he especially liked England and things English. He had studied medicine in London and returned to Peking to establish a clinic.

More happy years then with Emily never thinking of the misery throughout China, the quarrels between Communists and Nationalists, the incursions of the Japanese in the North, none of it penetrated the comfortable and cheerful circle of her new home. She taught the son, Lu Chen, and the daughter, Ma-Li, and helped the doctor with his English correspondence, often working as his secretary, and life had fallen into a safe and satisfying routine.

But no one realized, least of all Emily Chow, that China, with many a twist and turn and rough and dangerous way, was taking the first steps down a road to a new society—a society that hated and feared Westerners.

World War II began for China in 1937 when the Japanese began pushing down from the North. By 1939, the fighting was widespread and Dr Tang left Peking for the battlefields, trying to establish some minimal kind of health care for Chinese soldiers. In the northern provinces, the Chinese armies dispersed into the countryside to make guerilla attacks on the Japanese occupation troops. First aid stations for Chinese soldiers were makeshift huts or patched and deserted inns.

Chinese soldiers died by the millions, died of disease and starvation, dysentery and malaria. There were no corpsmen, no care for the wounded. Only walking wounded, dragging themselves, step by painful step, ever reached a doctor's care.

When Dr Tang came home to Peking in September 1945, Emily scarcely recognized him. His once thick black hair was lacklustre and streaked with grey, his plump face gaunt and wrinkled. Exhausted, ill with malaria, he lay close to death. Emily nursed him, begged quinine from old friends and one day, three weeks after his return, she found him sleeping quietly in the afternoon, his fever broken.

He heard her step. His eyes flickered open and he reached out a weak hand for her to hold. Then, realizing that at last he was home, he struggled to get up, but, try though he might, he was too weak to pull himself up.

Breathing heavily, his voice scarcely rising high enough for her to hear, he urged her to hurry, to gather up the children and go, to escape while there still was time.

She reassured him, told him the war was over. She smiled and reached for a fresh cloth to wipe his face, but he shook his head. He was angry now, weak and angry and desperate, and at last he made her understand that he knew the war with Japan was over.

"But the war for China is just beginning."

He knew. He had worked with the Communist armies in the North and he knew they would never stop until the peasant was free and the old China swept away.

And his heart was with them. But he saw, too, that there was no place in the China-to-come for those who had worked with the West, followed the West. No place for him or his family.

She and the two children left Peking that week, taking with them a sack of gold coins, coins that had lain hidden beneath a garden flagstone for eight years of war. Their goal was Hong Kong and, ultimately, the United States.

"It took us two years to reach Canton," she said simply. "The fighting, the horror of Civil War . . . I will not tell you the things we saw in those two years."

Ma-Li was thirteen, Lu Chen seventeen when they came to Canton. And Ma-Li was sick.

"I could not speak Cantonese. Everything was disrupted because of the fighting and we would be suspect to the Nationalist forces because we came from Peking. I found a room for us in a quiet part of the city. Ma-Li worsened. She was too sick to travel. I didn't know what to do for we were so close to Hong Kong.

Her voice faltered. Her decision, finally, as Ma-Li sank deeper into a fever, was to give Lu Chen half the gold coins. She found a fishing sampan whose owner agreed to carry him to Hong Kong. She told Lu Chen to find the Presbyterian Church in Hong Kong. She and Ma-Li would come there.

The sampan left before dawn one August morning. She watched the sun come up and spill like liquid gold across the Pearl River delta. She watched until she could no longer see the low squat outline of the sampan.

Ma-Li rallied toward the end of the week, lifted her head and smiled and managed to eat some beef broth. Smiling, she slipped back into sleep and then the fever returned. She died two weeks and one day after her brother left.

"I searched for Lu Chen in Hong Kong for five years," Miss Chow said quietly. Finally, with little hope, she had come to America. It was there that Dr Tang had wished for them to come.

It was in 1952 that she arrived in San Francisco, carrying with her the ashes of Ma-Li. Miss Chow found a job as a housekeeper with a wealthy Mandarin family that had fled the Communist mainland. She worked and periodically visited the Presbyterian mission in Chinatown and regularly, twice a year, placed a notice in two of the Chinese newspapers and in the *San Francisco Examiner* advertising for Lu Chen.

"But the years pass away," she said, "and there is never an answer. Did he ever reach Hong Kong or was he robbed and killed on the sampan? If he arrived in Hong Kong, was he tempted to stay on his own, to be a man alone? I don't know." She sighed. "I will never know."

But she kept his sister's ashes and continued to hope. Dr Tang had said he would come to America, find Emily and the two children.

It was in 1972, after China had once again opened her doors to America, that Emily Chow began to write to Peking. A letter to the Tang home. A letter to the hospitals. A letter to an old family friend. Finally, she dared to address the city government.

"I received an answer last week. I thought about it all week long. I suppose I have known in my heart for many years. But, still, I did not know what to do. So I asked Jimmy to come."

The city informed her, briefly, that Dr Tang had died in the great flu epidemic of 1948.

"All these years I have waited. Now it was time to arrange for Ma-Li's burial." She nodded toward the corner and I saw the small stone urn that she had guarded for so long. "And I wished to ask Jimmy if he felt I could in peace no longer advertise for Lu Chen. I would like to feel that I have done my duty."

Dan reached out to gently pat the hands that held so tightly now to the fluffy mass of knitting.

THIRTEEN

One more stop and we would complete our quest. I was discouraged now. We had talked to so many, walked so many blocks, looked into so many lives, and in none of them could I see a trace of Peking Man.

Annie at Self-Help for the Elderly, the Chan family in Ping Yuen, Yuan Lee's grief-stricken sister, jovial Buddy at the East Wind Restaurant, Miss Chow at the Green Door Hotel . . . I couldn't believe any of them had hidden the most famous fossils in history. Only the Middle Kingdom Gallery remained to be visited and its owner certainly wouldn't need help to sell Peking Man.

One more time we walked the length of Grant Avenue, passed the groceries, the laundries, reached the string of shops.

The minute we stepped inside the Middle Kingdom Gallery I felt sure we had made a mistake. This wasn't the kind of place to look for war booty. A magnificent silken tapestry hung against the wall to our right. An elegant rosewood dining table sat beneath it.

The sound of our shoes on the highly-waxed wooden floor sounded, to my ears, harsh and intrusive.

A curtain of beads rustled at the back of the room and a slender young woman in the distinctive Chinese dress, a side-slit cheong-sam, glided toward us, her soft black slippers making scarcely a sound.

I was sure suddenly that this was not the place for us. If Peking Man had been here, whoever owned this shop would not need Jimmy Lee to sell the fossils. Whoever owned all these beautiful works of art would well know the worth of Peking Man.

Jimmy must have come for another reason. I wanted to tug on Dan's sleeve, get us out of here, but he was already asking the girl about Jimmy, if she had talked to him yesterday.

She smiled and nodded. "Yes, he came just before we closed and talked to Mr Lee in his office."

Dan asked if we could see the owner. The girl disappeared through the beaded curtain and in a moment Mr Lee came out. He was as spare and elegant as his shop, tall and slender, almost attenuated arms and legs, like a grasshopper. As Dan talked, he hunched himself like a grasshopper, seemed to pull tightly into himself.

". . . like to know why Jimmy came here yesterday."

The overhead fluorescent light glittered on the owner's wire frame glasses and I couldn't see his eyes behind the thick lens. His bony sunken face never varied in expression from the beginning of Dan's words to their end.

There was a slight pause when Dan finished then the older man, he must have been fifty at least, began to shake his head.

"I am so sorry that I cannot help you. There must be a mis-understanding. Mr Jimmy Lee did not come to my humble store yesterday. It has not been my privilege to meet Mr Jimmy Lee."

Dan frowned.

There was an odd uncomfortable silence that stretched and spread. He was lying, Mr Wilkie Lee was lying! The girl must only have said that we wished to see him, not why.

The silence spread and gathered and grew. I looked at Dan. What was he going to do?

Mr Lee cleared his throat and the dry sharp sound was almost shocking in that heavy silence. Silence that pushed

and pressured and finally pulled reluctant words from Mr
Lee. "I am a very busy man, very busy this afternoon, I have
many things to do. If you do not wish to look at my poor objects then I must bid you . . ."

Dan interrupted and his voice was lazy and silky and I remembered going to an antique shop in a sleepy Arkansas
town once with my Great-Uncle Horace who collected Civil
War era photograph albums. There had been just that tone in
Uncle Horace's voice when he asked mildly how much the
dealer wanted, oh, for that box of junk over there, near the
door, the one with the milk eggs in it.

It wasn't the milk eggs he wanted, of course. It was the
half-seen weathered album with a velveteen backing and a
wooden front studded with rosettes of brass.

"Maybe I've gone about speaking to you in the wrong
way," Dan said. "I know that a man of business and especially
a man with your experience would understand that sometimes families will . . . have a little difference among themselves over how something of value in the family should be
sold."

Another silence.

Mr Lee's cadaverous face didn't change but his bony
shoulders moved a little. "I am always happy to appraise objects . . . of art, Mr Lee. If you will bring . . . whatever you
have to me, I will be happy to look at it." He nodded his head
once, twice. "I do not charge a fee to appraise. If we can work
out something advantageous to you then I will expect a small
commission. A commission that we can negotiate."

"That is very reasonable," Dan said agreeably. "I will get
back in touch with you, Mr Lee, when I am ready to dispose
of this . . . property."

When we were outside, away from the oppressive quiet of
the Middle Kingdom, when we were a block down Grant

Avenue, deep in the cover of an ordinary Chinatown crowd, tourists, little old ladies, hurried businessmen, I asked, "Dan, what possessed you to do that? Don't you see, you've warned him, made it impossible for us . . ." I broke off.

Dan took it up. "Impossible to do what?"

I shrugged. "Prove he talked to Jimmy."

"That's all right. We know that. At least, I'm dammed sure of it." He grinned. "Ellen, we're getting somewhere! I feel better than I have since this whole mess started. Until now it's been like boxing at shadows, nothing to take hold of, nothing to catch onto. But now . . . it's a whole new ball game. And little Dan's pitching. By God, we've got something started." He walked a little faster. "And you know what? I'm hungry! Come on, it's late but let's go get some lunch. At a Chinese restaurant."

He led the way up steep-pitched Sacramento to the Hang Ah tea room and introduced me to the delights of dim sum, a Chinese lunch. The waiter brought tray after tray and Dan selected one dish after another. We started with soft warm buns that enclosed different fillings, barbecued pork, a delicious mixture of peanut butter and sesame seeds, honey glazed pork, shrimp, then steamed dumplings of beef and chopped shrimp, crisp noodles with pork rind and the lightest fluffiest rice I had ever eaten.

We ate hungrily, talked quickly, and he didn't convince me.

"Okay," I agreed, "the man's a liar and it's obvious he talked to Jimmy. But we shouldn't have let him know we know that!"

"Sure we should," Dan answered.

"Why?"

"Because if he's the rat who sent those hoods after Jimmy then he's been warned that Jimmy isn't alone. That gives

119

Jimmy some protection until we find him."

"Maybe," I said grudgingly. "But the thing is, Dan, when you push a stick into a beehive, you're not only liable to stir up the bees, you're liable to get stung!"

But Dan wasn't really listening. He was figuring out loud how to find Jimmy.

"He's probably hiding not far from here." He frowned. "Hey, Ellen, all he had in that gym bag was one skull, wasn't it?"

"I think so."

"So the rest of the bones are wherever he found them, probably right here in Chinatown. Well, if Jimmy's trying to set up a deal to sell the fossils then he'll have to get all of them together." He finished his tea in a gulp. "Come on. That gives me some ideas."

His office was in the financial district in one of the glass and chrome office buildings on Kearney. The office window framed a brightly blue square of the Bay. Now, late afternoon, a white ship steamed slowly out to sea, soon to slip beneath the Golden Gate Bridge and pass out into the Pacific swells, bound perhaps for Hawaii or Japan or Mexico.

San Francisco, entryway to America for Orientals. Gum Sahn, the incoming Chinese had called it, Land of the Golden Mountains, lured by the promise of the goldfields a hundred years ago.

I turned back toward Dan. He sat at his desk, the telephone cradled between chin and shoulder, making call after call, trying to find some trace of Jimmy, alerting everyone to call Dan if they saw him. Dan looked at home behind his desk; he belonged, in his natural habitat, a legal pad, sharpened pencils, a dictaphone, an in box, an out box. A neat desk. A man with an orderly mind. A good lawyer, I felt confident. There is something about a good lawyer that sets him apart, a certain toughness and confidence and willingness to listen.

But I wondered if those were the best qualities to find Peking Man.

My eyes roamed the office. I felt comfortable. It reminded me of my father's office, orderly rows of books, the Pacific Reporters, California Statutes, the stacks of folders crammed with letters and documents, pleadings and contracts, interrogatories and depositions. Dan lived, worked in an orderly, reasonable, practical, sophisticated world.

I wasn't at all sure that was the same world Jimmy lived in. There was nothing orderly in Chinatown, lives out of kilter, lives turned upside down at the mercy of the dollar.

Anything could happen in Chinatown.

We had moved through it, knocked on doors, walked along crowded Grant Avenue, seen grief and despair and elegance, and I didn't think we were one step nearer those brownish mottled fossils.

I walked slowly across the office, stood beside Dan's desk. It was time to stop pretending we could handle it alone. Time to ask for help. Time to call the police.

Dan was still on the telephone, his pen scrawling across the yellow legal pad.

"You can count on me, Bill. You know I can keep my mouth shut. But this is important, damn important. It's . . . family, Bill." He listened, nodding, "Right . . . I understand . . . sure . . . big trouble, right . . . how much? . . . whew . . . I'll say . . . right, this is strictly confidential . . . listen, Bill, I appreciate it . . ."

When he hung up, he was exuberant. "Okay, Ellen, we're getting someplace now. We really are. Bill's on one of the Chinese newspapers and there's not much he doesn't know about Chinatown and everybody in it and he's got some real stuff on Mr Wilkie Lee. Our Mr Lee's in trouble, bad trouble. He's been gambling, running it up with the big boys, and he owes eighty-five thousand dollars."

Eighty-five thousand dollars. Even for the owner of a high-class shop, that kind of gambling debt was way out of sight.

Dan was saying so, too. "He probably looks rich to out-siders, but you know how it goes. He probably still owes a lot on the shop and has his money tied up in art goods. Now the gamblers are leaning on him. He's running out of time to pay up. If Jimmy tried to sell the fossils to him, it must have seemed like an answer from heaven—if he could get them gratis."

"You think that's what happened? That Jimmy tried to sell Peking Man to Mr Lee and that he decided to try and take the bones so he could get all the money for himself?"

"It makes sense," Dan answered. "We know Jimmy went to the Middle Kingdom Gallery. Lee denied seeing him. Why should he do that?"

I shrugged. People will do the damndest things. More to the point, what difference did it make what Wilkie Lee did if he didn't have the bones?

"Dan, none of this helps! I mean, who cares what kind of problems Lee has? Say he tried to highjack the bones. Well, so what? We're pretty sure he didn't get them. Jimmy got away from those guys so we aren't any closer to Jimmy or Peking Man!"

"We can't be sure," Dan said grimly. "Because . . . no-body's seen Jimmy."

So Dan was worried.

"Let's call the police," I said abruptly.

He looked surprised. "Earlier you were opposed to calling them. You said it might be more dangerous for Jimmy."

I turned away from the desk, paced back toward the

window. Yes, I had felt that. And, to be honest, I had felt that calling the police would bring more danger to Peking Man, too. If we loosed the world after Jimmy, it might not be the police who found him and the fossils first. But now I sensed that the longer Jimmy ran free, the less likely we were to recover Peking Man.

I swung back to face Dan. He was waiting for my answer and I could see the fear in the back of his black eyes. He didn't give a damn about Peking Man. And he assumed, of course, that I was putting Jimmy first, too. For an instant I hated myself, hated that instinctive scholar's protective response.

But, my God, the fossils would mean so much to man's history! To have them again, to be able to test and see if they were so much older than had been supposed, to study and measure and evaluate and, yes, to venerate because this was part of us, part of the magnificent natural heritage of mankind.

On the one hand Jimmy Lee, who had a good heart, and on the other the safety and protection of a great natural treasure.

I couldn't look into Dan's eyes. I turned away again, paced back to the window, answered him over my shoulder.

"I don't know." I said it angrily. "I just don't know."

"Hey, Ellen, don't be upset. We're making progress." His chair pushed back, he moved toward me. "And look, it does help that we've pitched on Wilkie Lee. He won't dare . . . hurt Jimmy now. And maybe this will give Jimmy a chance to get those damned bones sold, then everything will be all right."

I was gripping the edge of the window frame with one hand. My fingers ached, I held on so tightly.

That was the problem, of course. Everything would be all wrong as far as I was concerned. Because I owed a duty to myself, to my museum, to my profession to recover and protect those fossils. If I stood by, let them be raffled off, well, if it ever came out, I would be ruined.

"What are you going to do, Dan?" I was surprised at how evenly I asked, surprised that nothing in my voice betrayed me.

"See what else I can find out about Wilkie Lee. Then I may lean on him a little. See if I can find out what he does know. It might be enough to give us a better idea where Jimmy found the fossils."

I remembered Wilkie Lee's bony tight face. It would take a big lean to frighten him because he was already desperate.

"From what you said to him earlier, he must think you have the bones. That's what it sounded like."

"That's all right," Dan said confidently. "I can handle him."

It was nearing the end of a long day. I had walked into a lot of lives that day so perhaps it wasn't surprising that I knew both too much and too little to guess what might happen next.

But we should have had some inkling.

I had warned Dan that the fellow who stirs up the beehive is likely to be stung. I had sensed that. But I didn't think it through.

Dan and I were overlooking two vital facts.

We had mowed a wide swathe through Chinatown. A nearsighted gnat couldn't have missed it. How could we possibly think we could have escaped the notice of the persons who held those bones?

That was one fact.

The other was our absolute failure to consider what Jimmy was doing.

It was that too-human tendency to think ourselves the centre of creation, to take into account only what we are doing and planning and imagining. And to forget that the rest of the world not only doesn't give a damn but is pretty busy with its own pursuits.

I was very much involved in my own centric thoughts. About my career, my future, my responsibility—and just how much of a bastard I was willing to be.

If I blew the whistle, called in the cops . . .

Dan's voice made me jump. "Don't you think that's a good idea?"

"I'm sorry. I was . . . thinking. Is what a good idea?"

"Leaning on Wilkie Lee."

The light streaming through the window struck him full face. I could see the faint lines at the corners of his eyes and the creases that bracketed his mouth and would get deeper with age. His was a commanding, exciting, bold face but just now, looking down at me, I saw an edge of uncertainty and a willingness to share that uncertainty. It takes a particular kind of toughness to ask for help. He was asking me whether that was the best way to help Jimmy.

Not how to rescue Peking Man.

I owed him an honest answer. I owed him that at least.

"Yes," I managed, "yes, I think that is the best protection for Jimmy."

If we let well enough alone, if we alerted the police, set them to watch Wilkie Lee and the tough young men in his employ, they might capture Jimmy—and we might catch all of them and Peking Man, too.

But there was danger in that. Wilkie Lee's young men had knives and would, I didn't doubt, use them. The safest thing for Jimmy would be for Wilkie Lee's toughs to be drawn off, decoyed by Dan, while Jimmy made his move and, somehow, sold Peking Man.

Encouraged, Dan turned back to his desk.

I had followed Dan all day. He had looked for Jimmy and I

had looked for the faint trail of Peking Man. I didn't know, standing there in Dan's office, what I would have done had I found the fossils.

And I didn't know, standing there, watching him, seeing him look up and the quick smile in his eyes when he saw me watching, what I was going to do next.

FOURTEEN

Dan took me home to my apartment. We would go back to see Wilkie Lee in the morning, do a little leaning. Meanwhile, he would scout around, see if he could pick up anything more about Lee.

I didn't ask Dan to come in. He waited for a moment in the doorway then he thanked me and turned to go.

I wanted to call him back. I watched him walk away, watched him turn at the end of the hall and start down the stairs.

I didn't call him back.

Instead, I stepped inside, closed my door and leaned wearily against it. My apartment seemed strange. I felt that I had been gone a long, long time. I glanced at the clock. Just short of six. Was it only the night before that I had cleaned shrimp and rolled out cracker crumbs?

Almost six. Soon it would be twenty-four hours since I had held that incredible skull in shaking hands. Every second that passed, every minute and hour that I delayed, made it more likely that Peking Man would be bartered away like a sack of potatoes. And to what eventual end?

I pushed away from the door, began to walk slowly across the room to my desk . . . and my telephone. It is so easy to dial a telephone. I could dial seven numbers and talk to the police. Or the FBI. A few numbers more and I could reach Chicago or New York, alert the world to the re-emergence of Peking Man.

But, once I dialled, once I spoke, there would be no

turning back. Jimmy Lee would be in grave danger. Then it would not be only the police and scientists searching for him. The predators would be out, too, the wolflike, softpadded, clever and deadly predators.

I reached down, touched the cold plastic of the receiver. My hand moved away, straightened the onyx pen set that Richard had given me . . .

Richard! My God, he was coming to dinner! Tonight! I had forgotten, forgotten completely.

I did not want Richard to come to dinner.

All right, Ellen, you're a big girl, I told myself. You can speak up, communicate. Why the hell don't you call, tell him not to come?

I looked at the small clock on my desk. Richard would be here in fifty-five minutes. I couldn't call now, at this late hour, and tell him I didn't want him to come to dinner. I couldn't make an excuse two nights in a row.

Fifty-five minutes. No time then to call anyone about Peking Man, no time for anything if I were to be ready in time. I needed a shower, fresh clothes, and, Lord love us, a magician's wand in the kitchen. No casserole, of course. Instead, I'd make a lemon sauce for the broccoli and serve the avocados open with a splash of dressing. The crackers were already rolled out and the shrimp cleaned so that would be easy.

I needed to hurry, to get started, but still I stood by my desk. I should call Richard and tell him not to come.

What kind of game was I playing?

Self-encounters never happen conveniently. But, sometimes, you have to stop, pin yourself down, brush past presence and convention, divine the reason, not the rationalization.

It wasn't southern courtesy that kept me from cancelling

our dinner. There are so many soft-voiced ways to renege. It wasn't a commitment to Richard. If it were Richard's welfare that moved me, indeed, perhaps I should cancel our dinner.

I jerked around, hurried across the room, but I carried that cold still search for truth within me. In my narrow bedroom, I paused beside my dresser and reached down to touch lightly the fragile handpainted antique china powder box that Richard had given me for Christmas.

He had watched as I opened the gaily-wrapped package and my soft oh of pleasure had delighted him. I had looked up and his blue eyes were warm and smiling—and we were, at that moment, very close.

Tonight I didn't want him to come for dinner.

I undressed hurriedly, plunged into a shower, soaped, washed. As I stepped out onto the mat and began to towel, I thought, it's only fatigue, that's all it is.

If you love someone, you don't push him away when you are tired. That's the time to reach out . . .

I saw Dan's face suddenly, the sharp angles of his cheeks, his mouth, his smooth honey dark skin, his vivid black eyes.

Five minutes to dress, lemon slacks, a white silk blouse, lemon scarf, white sandals, then into the kitchen.

I yanked the cracker crumbs and shrimp out of the refrigerator, lifted two eggs from the rack. As I worked, everything began to slip into better focus. I liked Richard. I had been, these past few months, near to loving Richard.

It would be idiotic to let a twenty-four hour escapade, a brief violent plunge into an alien world, destroy something that had grown and built slowly, steadily, comfortably.

I dropped another shrimp into the egg batter then plucked it, dripping, to roll in cracker crumbs.

I would tell Richard about Peking Man . . . But could I? He would be appalled that I hadn't notified the authorities! He would never understand my hesitation.

But, if I couldn't tell Richard about Peking Man, couldn't go to him for help in making that decision, then we didn't have, between us, the kind of honesty that love demands.

With Richard or without, I must decide. Delaying was only another kind of decision—and a weak-willed one. Right now, this instant, before Richard came, I must decide whether to call the police, set in motion the public search for Peking Man, or whether to run with Jimmy, to keep quiet and let him sell to anyone he chose a treasure that by rights belonged to the world.

I turned in the hot water, rinsed my hands and was drying them when a knock sounded at my front door.

Startled, I looked at the kitchen clock. Six-fifty. Of all nights for Richard to be early! I hurried to the door, damning Richard and totting up what still needed to be done. Well, I would put him to work. He could set the table while I made the sauce for the broccoli.

I even managed a smile as I began to open the door. Then my smile turned to a gasp of pain as the door slammed viciously into me, jolting my arm and shoulder, knocking me backward and off-balance.

Those old-young frightening faces, empty of expression, neither angry nor excited nor even very interested. Vacuous and stolid and utterly dangerous, they moved together, the shorter one shutting the door behind them, the thin wiry one reaching out to grab me.

I bounced off one end of the couch and managed to elude him, lunging frantically to my right.

Why me? My God, I'm afraid, afraid. Those hands, I didn't want those hands to touch me. I tried to scream but it was the hissing gasp of a frightened rabbit.

The wiry one caught me at the door to the kitchen. His

arms closed around me and I hated the feel of his body against my back and the brutal pressure of his hands on my arms.

I struggled and squirmed and tried to kick but he only held me tighter.

It all happened so quickly and in silence, our quick panting breaths and the scuff of our shoes against the wooden floor the only sounds of my struggle.

The solid knock on the door arrested time and movement as sharply as a camera freezes, stills forever, its subject.

My head twisted toward the door and my temple was taut against my captor's chin. I could smell his breath, sour, to-bacco-bitter, and feel the hard bristles on his cheek.

The knock sounded again.

The stocky young man, the one I had whanged with a claw hammer the night before, still stood near the door. There was danger in the way he stood, leaning forward just a little, ready to spring, violent, savage. His hands darted inside his jacket and out again and the knife was an extension of his hand, a predator's natural weapon.

The knock came again, hesitant now.

Oh Richard, what did you think, standing in that familiar hallway? A gentleman always, what could you possibly think? I'd broken our date last night. If you called me today, there was no answer. What could you think but that I'd forgotten?

"Ellen?"

His voice came faintly through the sturdy door. He wouldn't shout, of course. Not Richard.

If I screamed, if I managed one short desperate high-pitched scream . . .

The eyes of the youth at the door flickered toward me and my captor then back again to the door. He moved a step closer. Richard would not have a chance.

131

My captor shifted his grip and his right hand, smelling of machine oil and dust, fastened over my mouth and he pulled, arching my head backwards.

Still, if I jerked sharply, cried out, there should be breath enough for Richard to hear.

It was hard to breathe with his hand clamped against my mouth and nose, pulling, smothering.

Richard knocked again.

If they took me from my apartment, carried me out into the night as their captive, I would have no chance at all. There would not be, wherever they took me, anyone to hear my cries, anyone to help me. Anyone to care.

Richard did care. I knew that. He would do his best for me. He was a gentle man, a civilized man. Had he ever struck anyone? I doubted it. As a boy, he would have moved quietly in an orderly world. Danger is a choice, conscious or not. Teenagers who roam mean streets, drink in shabby bars, carry tyre chains after a football game, they find danger because they look for it. Richard had told me of his job after school in a shoe store. He had not walked late night streets.

If I cried out . . .

"Ellen?"

Oh Richard, I might have loved you still. I might have. I wasn't sure. But, love or not, I couldn't cry out, see you hurt, see you crumple before me, cut down by that deadly remorseless young man who waited, the knife easy in his hand.

I wanted to cry out. I so desperately wanted to scream for help.

Then my body sagged hopelessly against my captor's. I could hear so clearly, so unmistakably, the harsh clip of Richard's shoes as he strode away from my door.

He would not come back. He would be safe.

And I was alone with my enemies.

FIFTEEN

Blinded, gagged, hands tied tightly behind me, I never saw the van that carried me. I knew from the chill of the metal floor and the slam of the rear door that it was a van.

I lay as they dropped me, a heavy dusty moving pad covering me, as the van lurched out of the alley behind my apartment. How much time did I have? God knew. More than likely very little. Awkwardly, I rolled up on one elbow, shrugged the pad away from me. Panic washed over me. I couldn't see and the gag threatened to choke me. I knew I had to get loose. When they opened the door at our destination, that would be my last chance, my very final chance to break free, scream, attract attention. And I couldn't do it gagged.

I was on my knees now, shaking the pad away from me, trying to get to my feet. The van was pulling up a steep hill and, without hands to brace me, I couldn't balance on the tilting floor.

Time, Ellen, time!

To hell with getting up, just get there. I began to move on my knees, struggling like a penitente toward the rear of the van. I had a muzzy hope of standing at the back and trying to hook the gag and the blindfold on a door hinge and pull them off.

The van swung sharply left and I toppled to one side. I took the force of the fall on my shoulder. A wave of sickness swept over me but, once again, I got up on my knees and moved ahead. I even managed to stay upright when the van made another turn. I reached the back and, using my elbow

133

as an awkward support, began to stand. Bracing against the side wall, I used my cheek to hunt for the protruding hinge.

For an instant, I felt a surge of hope and a quick thrill of pleasure in my planning. There was the hinge. Now, if I could hook the taut strip of dishtowel that gagged me, then I would be able . . .

It was a lazy casual shove. Just enough to topple me backwards. As I fell, I realized, shockingly, that one of them was in the back of the van with me, that he had watched my useless struggle and waited until the last instant before striking me down.

With no hands to reach out and break my fall, I knew I was going to be hurt, no matter how I tried to twist and turn.

My head cracked painfully into the metal side of the van. Pain spread like a live thing down my neck and into my shoulder. I sagged gracelessly onto the floor, struggling to breathe as I fought the shock and the brackish taste of blood and the bitterness of defeat.

I lay in an awkward heap, too much in pain to care. I don't know how much longer the van rumbled up and down hills. I made no move when the motor finally stopped. Unable to see, unable to make more than a gasping sound, I had no more hope.

The rear door opened and the van floor dipped as the driver climbed up. Then the two of them shoved me roughly over onto the moving pad and rolled me up like a sausage in a pancake. Now, blindfolded, gagged, immobile and completely hidden, they swung me up and carried me out.

Dimly, I could hear the sounds of cars passing, the slam of the van door, shoes clicking on pavement, the screech of a door opening. Then my padded prison tilted and I heard the hollow sound of feet striking wooden steps and knew I was being carried downstairs.

Another door creaked open, shoes gritted again on cement. They dropped me on my back without warning but the moving pad absorbed most of the impact.

The door creaked shut.

My heart thudded painfully. I was now well and truly lost. I felt the beginnings of panic, the desire of a maddened animal to twist and pull and scratch my way to freedom, knowing all the while that it would do no good, that the harder I strained, the tighter my bonds would get. I knew it, I tried to hold to that understanding, tried to keep a bar of reason between myself and hysteria, yet, all the while, I felt my back beginning to arch, my muscles to strain.

The sound just reached me, just barely. It was so muted, that thin almost inhuman sound, that I barely heard it, but, when I did, I knew it for what it was—a moan of pain.

I lay absolutely still and listened, trying to hear over the thudding of my heart.

There was no other sound, nothing, not the scuff of footsteps or the slam of a door or even the faraway rattle of cars in the street. Nothing. Just the beating of my heart and the thick smothery warmth of the moving pad and the tickle of dust in my nose.

Then, faintly, the moan sounded again.

I began to rock back and forth, trying to loosen the moving pad. I was rolled up in it. I should be able to unroll. Sweat oozed down my sides, slipped down my legs. Back and forth, harder and harder I rocked but the pad seemed only to tighten around me. Farther, farther, then I was turning over and, abruptly, the pad pulled free beneath me. I kicked until I was free of it.

I rested for a moment and once again listened.

The moan, faint and high, didn't have a conscious sound and the sick feeling inside me grew.

I patted the cement floor behind me. I needed something sharp and stationary to try and cut free of the ropes that tied my hands. Using one elbow for support, I wriggled around and up on my knees and then to my feet. I stood unsteadily, uncertain what to do next for, of course, I couldn't see. I decided to step cautiously backward with my bound hands poked out behind me like stunted antennae.

Three uncertain paces back and I came up against the wall. It was of brick and fairly rough but nothing protruded enough to snag my blindfold.

Once again came that low pain-ridden moan.

I began to slide along the wall and had only gone a foot or two when I came up against something hard and wooden. Turning my back to it, my fingers felt the sleekness of lacquered wood. My hands moved up and down the edge at the front.

The hinges that supported the cabinet doors were small but they did protrude. I hooked my blindfold onto the hinge, then, slowly, steadily I began to pull down. The blindfold resisted, tightened around my head, then, abruptly, pulled free.

I could have wept in dismay.

The room was totally dark. I could see no more than before. For a long moment, I leaned wearily against the chest. Then, once again, that low faint moan.

The skin on my back prickled.

Who was it? Who was in that dark room with me? Who moaned in pain?

There had to be a light switch. If I kept on moving along the wall, found a door, a light switch should be near. I was tired and frightened of what the light might show. But I had to know.

Patiently, I moved along the wall, skirting out to pass obstacles such as the chest, until I reached the doorframe. I found the switch, reached it awkwardly with my hands behind me, and turned on the light.

I made a whimpering noise deep in my throat when I saw him. Mercifully, he was unconscious. That recurring sigh of pain came from deep inside, the body's uncontrolled lament.

I had never before seen anyone who had been deliberately hurt. Accidents, yes. The horror of a broken leg, the bone protruding, on a ski slope. A hand burned by spilled grease. But, never before the deliberate torture of one human being by another.

I wanted to cry out to Jimmy, wanted to help him.

His feet touched the ground, but he was unconscious, his body slumping forward, hanging from the rope that bound his wrists and suspended him from one of a row of large hooks that studded the low ceiling.

But I didn't look at his lacerated wrists or his head that dangled loosely forward between his upright arms.

I looked at his back.

Raised red welts crisscrossed his bared skin. On the right lower back, just beneath the ribcage, his skin was pulpy, so many welts that it was a mass of bloody disfigured tissue.

The top of his pants was thick with blood, crusted with blood.

My eyes dropped to the floor, to the strip of cord that lay in a heap. It was white nylon cord, no larger in diameter than a pencil, no longer than five feet. Two feet of it weren't white any more.

That beaten bloodied back moved up and down as he breathed. Slowly, so slowly. I had to get him down, ease some of the strain on that tortured body. I looked frantically around the basement room. I needed something sharp to cut me free.

It was a storeroom of sorts, filled mostly with furniture

that needed repair. One panel of the lacquered chest that I had used to pull off my blindfold was badly scarred. A heavy rosewood chair with a missing leg leaned against a waterstained table. Chairs, tables, smaller chests, rattan pieces, all were stacked haphazardly against the walls and out into the centre of the room.

Past Jimmy, the corner of the room was shadowy and seemed oddly lopsided, as if it had spread sideways. I leaned forward, straining to see, then began to walk.

A little alcove opened off the main storeroom. This was where the repair work was done. A toolbench ran the length of the nook. Above it hung files, chisels, hammers and a host of tools I didn't know.

I almost fell, I ran so quickly to the toolbench. We were saved, Jimmy and I. I had already spotted the best tool for me, a foot-long file with sharply abrasive sides. I would get the file . . .

I could not reach it. I could not lift my bound hands high enough behind me to touch the hanging tools. The tool bench was the proper height for someone to stand and work. I could not, no matter how hard I strained, I could not pull myself up and onto the bench.

Something to stand on, that would do it! I hurried back into the main storeroom and laboriously began to drag a small table behind me toward the alcove.

I had no warning. The cellar was sturdily built, its door well fitted. The door swung inward and its creak was my only notice.

I swung around to face the door and my heart began its familiar thudding.

How old were they, the two of them? Surely not more than nineteen or twenty. Of an age with Jimmy. So young and so frightening; empty faces, cold eyes.

They looked at me and for the first time I saw something move in the eyes of the stocky blunt-faced leader. I took a step backwards.

He saw that and laughed, a light breathless laugh that sent a prickle down my back.

"Take it easy, lady. All we want is a little cooperation, that's all."

Easy voice, easy words. Nothing threatening there. Then he turned to his wiry smaller companion and made a little gesture, nodded his head toward me.

I knew, knew with a horrid certainty, that something terrible was going to happen. But, at first, I didn't understand what. Not at first.

The thin boy didn't look at me. He circled behind me and I felt the tugging at the ropes and realized he was cutting the cord from my wrists. As my hands fell free, he grabbed my arm, pushed me ahead of him until we were close to Jimmy.

The stocky one was beside us now, too, the three of us so close to Jimmy who dangled there, his breathing heavy. The thin boy yanked my hands in front of me and the stocky one began to wind cord around them. It wasn't until the cord was tight and they abruptly lifted me, pulling my arms up and jamming the taut cord over one of the ceiling hooks, that I understood.

I began to struggle, twisting, pulling, kicking. My left heel caught the skinny one's knee and he yelped. Stumbling back, he began to swear and then, without any warning, his fist smashed into my stomach.

The gag muffled my scream. Nausea bubbled in my throat but I knew I must not be sick or I would choke. And, over the sickness and the pulsing pain in my stomach, was the slimy whispering rush of fear. What were they going to do to me? What were they going to do?

I knew, with the sensitivity of fear, that they had moved away from me, behind me.

"Get some water, yeah, some water."

I knew his voice now, the sound of the stocky one. He spoke the way he laughed, a breathless light voice.

My chest still heaved as I tried to get enough air, tried not to vomit, and tried, too, to figure out what they were doing behind me.

A water faucet was turned on, ran for a moment, then twisted off. Water splashed and dripped close behind me and I realized they were trying to wake Jimmy up.

To hurt him more?

"Yeah, man, time to wake up." It was the stocky one talking, his voice light and feathery. "Yeah, good man, come on now, wake up. Tell you what, man, we're gonna cut you down even though you haven't been so helpful. But it's all right now 'cause we got somebody new."

He grabbed my hair, pulled my head around until I was looking over my shoulder.

Jimmy stared. For a long moment, there wasn't even a hint of recognition then, slowly, painfully, he shook his head. "Oh no, no."

"What's the lady's name, Jimmy boy?"

Jimmy closed his eyes, turned his face away.

"The lady's name." That light feathery voice and its undercurrent of viciousness.

The only sound was Jimmy's laboured breathing. And, without warning, my scream, only partially muffled by the gag.

He yanked my hair, pulling my head back until the strain on my neck was intolerable. Through my pain and panic, I heard that light feathery voice, "The lady's name, Jimmy."

"Dr Christie." A broken whisper. "Dr Christie."

140

He held my head back a moment longer then let go.

"That's nice. That's much better. Now listen close, Jimmy, it will save all of us a lot of trouble. Not that Harry minds a little trouble."

Harry. The skinny one. I twisted my head, looked back, and a hot sick wave of fear crawled over me. Harry held loosely in his hands that length of cord that had lain on the floor near Jimmy, the cord with the bloodied end.

Jimmy, his face dogged, wouldn't look at the stocky one.

"Where are the bones, Jimmy? All you have to do is tell us where the bones are."

Jimmy shook his head, back and forth, back and forth.

The stocky one walked around, began to cut loose my gag. "Dr Christie, here, she's going to want you to tell us, Jimmy. She's going to want you to tell us real bad."

He was tugging my blouse up and out of my slacks, pulling it up to my shoulders. I saw Harry moving behind me, that bloodied length of cord dangling from his upraised fist.

SIXTEEN

I knew, that frightful instant, that it was coming. I saw the muscles move in his arm, saw his hand tighten, saw the reddened cord begin to make its whistling descent, saw and began to twist and pull, but there was no escape.

A whitehot line of flame seared my back.

I heard my cry from a distance, heard that explosive uncontrollable pain-wracked sound, knew that I had made it, and felt, over the pain and the fear, a kind of shame. That couldn't be me, not Ellen Christie, not that animal-like shriek.

Jimmy called out, "No, don't, don't, I'll tell you, no . . ."

But still the cord whipped through the air, harder now, and the haze of pain was even greater than the fear and sickness and I writhed and squirmed, my wrists burning, pulling against the ropes, trying somehow, anyhow, to move away from the hurt.

I just heard the sharp order and sensed the stocky one moving between me and Harry. My chest heaved and my back was alive with a thousand tentacles of agony.

"I'll tell you, you bastard, but get her down first. Get her down."

"Sure, Jimmy. Sure thing. And you, too."

He lifted me up, unhooked my wrists, even put out a hand to steady me. Then he turned to Jimmy, unhooked him. But Jimmy couldn't stand and crumpled to the cement floor. I moved unsteadily but determinedly and knelt by him.

"It's all right." Jimmy rested on his knees, his head bent

forward, then, taking a deep breath, he looked up. "Okay, I'll tell you where the bones are. But I don't want the person who has them hurt. I'm going to give you a letter to her so she'll trust you, give you the fossils. You won't have to hurt her." He looked at Harry and his voice shook. "I swear, if you hurt her, I'll kill you. Somehow. I'll kill you."

They moved a little, the two of them. "All we want is the bones."

Jimmy nodded. He squinted at them, then asked, "What time is it?"

"What's it to you?" the stocky one asked.

Jimmy was impatient. "It makes a difference."

"It's almost ten."

"Ten at night, huh?"

The stocky one nodded.

"It's too late tonight then. Take the letter, go see her in the morning. She won't suspect anything then." He sighed. "All right, get me some paper, a pen."

He stared at the sheet when they brought it, stared for a long moment, then began to write.

I saw him write the name and felt a flutter of excitement and shock but, somehow, no surprise. We should have known, we really should have known.

Jimmy paused after a moment, then looked up at our stocky captor, "What's your name?"

He didn't answer.

"Look," Jimmy said, "I have to put down a name, some name."

The young man hesitated then said, "Ted. Ted Wong."

It wouldn't, of course, be his real name. But it was a name. Jimmy wrote some more, then read it over, signed it, handed it up to 'Ted'.

'Ted' read it aloud in his light feathery voice, "Dear Miss

Chow, Please give the container with the fossils to Ted Wong, the bearer of this note. He is to be trusted. I will be in touch with you shortly. Your faithful friend, Jimmy Lee." He looked down at Jimmy. "It sounds okay. And it will save her some trouble if she thinks we're friends and hands them over." He smiled, a little thin smile. "You better hope she antes up, Jimmy boy."

Before leaving, they took another cord, slipped it through the cord that bound our wrists and tethered us, like whipped dogs, to a central post. So the tools in the alcove might as well have been on the moon for all the good they could do us.

And I turned out not to be too proud to ask a favour. They were at the door, the stocky one reaching out for the light switch.

"Please," I said, "will you leave the light on?"

He looked back, shrugged, left it on. That was something. Not a lot, but something.

The door clicked shut. What would they do now? Wait until morning to go to the Green Door? I thought they might. They could slip in early tomorrow, knock, show her the letter and hope to get the fossils without any trouble. If they went tonight, they would have to knock loud enough to awaken her. She might not answer her door at night and too much noise would immediately attract all kinds of attention in the crowded hotel.

So we were likely to be left alone until morning. Surely we could get loose. Or, if not free, maybe we could make noise. But that would draw our captors. I wasn't making much sense, even to myself. I turned to ask Jimmy what he thought and was stricken by the way he slumped, resting his arms and face on his knees.

"Jimmy, does it hurt dreadfully!"

I thought at first he hadn't heard, but, finally, he lifted his head and it was desolation I saw in his face, not suffering. "I should have known anybody greedy enough to kick forty-three old people out into the gutter was no goddam good at all." He stopped and his mouth quivered. "Dan told me I was a chump when I quit school. Well, I guess he was right. Dumb Jimmy. Jimmy the cluck. But I never thought he would try to take the bones for nothing! It was a good deal for him, the fossils for the Green Door."

I tried to make some sense out of his bitter words.

"Who, Jimmy? And what does the Green Door have to do with any of it?"

"The Green Door," he repeated. "Oh God, what's going to happen to all of them! Old and alone and no place to go and nobody to give a damn! Nobody. And I was so sure it would work out. But I should have known that nothing's ever easy if a lot of money is involved because somebody always gets greedy. If he weren't a greedy bastard to begin with, he wouldn't be trying to sell the Green Door."

"Who, Jimmy?"

"Wilkie Lee."

Everything shifted then, came clear and sharp and coldly logical. Wilkie Lee owned the Green Door Hotel and the Middle Kingdom Gallery and it must have made perfect sense to Jimmy to try and trade the fossils for the hotel. But Jimmy didn't know just how badly Wilkie Lee needed money.

When I told him, he shook his head back and forth. "I could have gone a dozen different ways," and his voice was heartsick. "I took just the one skull from Miss Chow and went back to Trouble, Inc. It was late afternoon and Lily was out making calls. I sat there at my desk and typed up the places I'd been, I'd forgotten to put it down before I left in the morning . . ."

I interrupted. "So that's why the list showed the Middle Kingdom Gallery last." I told him how we'd found Trouble, Inc a shambles, Lee's thugs must have broken in Wednesday night searching for the bones, and how Lily had found the list for us and we had followed Jimmy's trail through Chinatown.

"We didn't understand why you would go from the East Wind to the Green Door then back to the Middle Kingdom Gallery. But, the answer, of course, is that you didn't decide to visit the Gallery until after you had been to the hotel, which also meant you must have returned to the office Thursday evening and listed the places you had visited that day."

At least my insistence that Dan and I follow the list had kept Miss Chow safe until now for Lee's thugs must have followed Dan and me after we left the Gallery. They would have followed us to Dan's office and then again when he took me home and decided, perhaps, that it would be easier to grab a woman than Dan.

Dan and I should have known that it was Miss Chow who had the fossils. She and Buddy Wu were the only ones in charge of their lives—and Buddy wouldn't need help to sell anything.

"Miss Chow," Jimmy said softly, "she's really something else! She still works part-time, at one of the sewing factories, then spends her afternoons doing volunteer work at the Chinese Hospital—and she's seventy-two." His mouth twisted. "She should have called somebody besides me. I screwed it up good!"

"Don't say that, Jimmy!" I said sharply. "That's self-pity. And it doesn't help anybody."

His head jerked up at that. It was cruel, but it brought a flush to his face and that was better than the dull look of despair.

"Tell me how you found out about the fossils, what you did," I said briskly. It was better to talk and to listen. Silence compounds fear.

Miss Chow had called him the week before and asked him to come by. It was true enough that she had finally received an answer to Dr Tang's fate, but it wasn't a question of advertising for the son or disposing of the daughter's ashes that had made her call Jimmy.

It was to ask what she should do with a 'treasure' that had been entrusted to her by the doctor, to be kept safe until he found them in America.

Miss Chow had not described the 'treasure'. Jimmy had looked around the tiny room at the Green Door, at the narrow bed and orange-crate cabinets, and had been sure that whatever memento she had managed to bring the long way from China had grown in value in her mind over the years.

"I had told her that obviously whatever she had was now hers alone to do with as she pleased. That she had in every way fulfilled her obligations to the Tang family."

She had nodded and thanked him gravely, said she wished to think about her decision and asked him to return the coming Thursday.

"That was yesterday." He said it almost uncertainly, then nodded to himself. Yes, it had been only yesterday.

She welcomed him with green tea and only when he held the handleless cup in both his hands and had taken several sips and they had spoken of many things, his family, her work at the hospital, the lovely February weather, had she come to the point.

Jimmy looked a little embarrassed. "She told me she thought I had a good heart. Then she got up and went to her bed and stooped down to pull out this metal container."

147

She put the container on the bed and motioned for him to come close. At his first sight of the bones, he was more puzzled than excited. He poked them with a hesitant finger, handfuls of teeth, pieces of jaw, skull fragments, four thigh-bones and three almost complete skulls. But he began to understand when she said, "It's Peking Man."

"How did Dr Tang get the fossils?" I asked. "Did she know?"

"Toward the end of the war, Dr Tang operated on a general in one of the guerilla camps. He did it under fire and stayed and helped nurse the general back to strength. The day before he left the camp, the general called him to his tent, gave him a heavy khaki backpack. The bones were in it. Dr Tang knew what they were the minute he saw them. The general felt his luck was out and he wanted to repay Dr Tang. He told the doctor that he'd bought them from a Japanese colonel. There was a lot of dealing between the Chinese and Japanese for oil and guns, that sort of thing. Not a lot of honour on either side. The general said he got the best of the deal because he paid the colonel in Chinese paper money and, by 1945, a bushel of it wasn't worth much. The colonel tried to bargain for gold but he didn't try too hard. He was nervous, said too many people were looking for the bones and he'd take his chances on the paper money."

If the colonel had been in charge of the soldiers who rifled Camp Holcomb and he had held onto the bones and then heard that the Japanese Army secret police were quizzing the American prisoners about the bones, he might well have been nervous.

From a Japanese colonel to a Chinese general to a battlefield surgeon to a children's nurse—to Jimmy Lee. Oh yes, that could well have been the way of it.

And now, to a greedy desperate man?

"Miss Chow wanted you to sell the bones?"

Jimmy nodded.

"But what does the Green Door Hotel have to do with selling the bones?"

"Everything. She knew, you see, that the Green Door was up for sale. All of them knew it, I think. That's the kind of secret that can't be kept. And Bobby might have told her. Anyway, she knew the Green Door was going to be sold and she knew it belonged to Wilkie Lee. She had heard he was going to sell it for $145,000."

She told him that, then looked expectantly at Jimmy. He hadn't understood. He stared at the brownish yellow bones then back at Miss Chow.

"She said, 'The bones are worth more than that'. She knew to a penny what the bones were worth!" Jimmy almost laughed except that he hurt too much to laugh and nothing was funny now. "She had a damn scrapbook, would you believe? It was full of clippings about Peking Man. Lots of stories on Christopher Janus, the man in Chicago who's offered cash on the hoof. She pointed out the figures to me and, in one story, somebody estimated the fossils could bring as much as $250,000.

"Then she asked me very anxiously if I thought that would be a proper thing to do, to sell the bones and buy the Green Door. Her eyes blinked very quickly and she said some of them, the people who lived there, some of them were so frightened."

He looked at me and there was heartbreak in his eyes because now there was no longer any way to save their world, to keep forty-three old and poor and frightened people from being thrown out on the street. No place to go. No one to care.

"I thought it was going to be so easy," Jimmy said bitterly. He was sure it would work out. He took the skull and went to the Middle Kingdom Gallery. "I thought he would snap it up, but then he hemmed and hawed around, said he'd think about it, that he'd be in touch with me. But I saw him reach under his desk and I wondered. It was too much like a croupier's buzzer. That's when I began to get nervous and it came to me that if somebody highjacked the lot, well, I didn't have a Bill of Sale, you know. So I told him he'd better think fast 'cause I was leaving. He tried to keep me but I was on my way. I hit the street and heard the door slam behind me and it was those guys." I didn't have to ask which guys.

He began to run then, darting and twisting down Grant then dodging up Sacramento and hiding behind the children's playground as the two of them loped on up to Stockton. Then Jimmy ran across to the YM and stuck the skull in his locker.

That was when he had decided to check the bones out himself and, remembering the bone lady story, had come to my museum and followed me home.

My mind had gone on ahead, to Dan bursting into the basement and demanding to know what Jimmy was up to.

"When they lost you, they must have decided to watch Dan, hoping he would lead them to you. It's a small enough town that they could figure out who your brother was. And it worked."

Jimmy nodded.

"How did you get away from them?" I asked.

"They tangled with you and Dan long enough to give me a head start. And believe me, I didn't wait around for them once I got outside. I got my cycle and rode out to Berkeley and spent the night with, uh, with a friend. And sh . . . my friend let me stay all day today."

I wondered briefly who she was but that wasn't any business of mine.

"How did they catch you tonight?"

"I had to come back to Chinatown to get the rest of the fossils," Jimmy said wearily. "Miss Chow doesn't have a phone and I was afraid to call the hotel number and ask for her. I didn't know who might listen. I was so close to working everything out that I didn't want to take any chances." He twisted his wrist to look at his watch. "Eleven o'clock. Oh goddam, eleven o'clock!"

Eleven o'clock. 5am. Noon. What possible difference could it make? I asked him.

He looked at me wildly, began to pull on his ropes even though he knew it was hopeless. "Oh damn, don't you see! The parade is tomorrow night! Everthing's set and here we sit."

"What parade?"

He looked at me as if I were the crazy one. "Oh hell Dr Christie."

"Ellen." I interrupted automatically.

". . . Ellen, it's the big Chinese New Year parade. At seven tomorrow night. It starts at Pine and the Battery and winds through the financial district then up Grant to Bush and down Bush. It's spectacular, forty-fifty-sixty foot dragons, held by hand, you know. They have lights along the spines and they curl and curve up and downhill. It draws the biggest crowd of anything that happens all year. Two-three hundred thousand people jam the streets. That's why I thought it would be safe."

"Safe for what?"

"To meet the guy who's going to buy the fossils."

And Jimmy pulled again on his ropes.

SEVENTEEN

But no matter how Jimmy strained, those ropes weren't going to give. Tied up we were and tied up we were going to stay.

No matter how bad something is, no matter how scared you are, you still get tired and we both finally drifted into uneasy restless sleep. But not a deep sleep.

I woke first, heard the noise first, a muffled thumping chipping sound.

"Jimmy!"

It is terrible to be afraid. And we were both afraid. We looked toward the door but it was still closed. We looked around the dimly-lit room. Furniture crowded the walls, broken chairs and tables, rattan work of all kinds. We looked and listened.

It was a scratchy picky sound.

We had not, until now, heard any noise at all in this cellar room. No street sounds, nothing. So this odd continuing noise had to mean something.

Hope can be a terrible thing, too. Neither of us put it into words but our eyes searched the walls, the floor, strained to see in shadowy corners.

I saw the flicker of movement near the cabinet I had used to remove my blindfold. A dull flash, gone as soon as I saw it. But I did see it.

"Jimmy, look!"

A dry skittery crumbling sound now as fragments of mortar were pushed free to slither and fall down the wall. There had been a door there once, years ago, and it had been taken out and the space bricked up, a thick oblong whitish-grey band of mortar marking its place.

Behind me, I heard the soft coo of a pigeon. Startled, I swung around. It was Jimmy. He made the sound twice more then leaned forward, listening, and I saw the hope on his face.

Dimly, just audible, came an answering coo, once, twice, three times. He didn't have to tell me. It was Dan. Somehow, some miraculous way, it was Dan.

But it was taking so long. Time was running out. It was morning now, just past nine o'clock. Had they been to the Green Door yet, talked to Miss Chow? If they had, they might come back at any time. Although, if they now had the fossils, they might not be in any hurry to get to us, might, in fact, want to wait until dark to spirit us away from here.

Jimmy and I didn't have to talk that one over, either. We both began to study the objects stacked and balanced near the door. A narrow seven-shelfed bookcase sat to the left of the door and a huge dining room table of rosewood to the right.

"Hey, Ellen, if we could reach that bookcase with our feet and give it a hard shove, tip it to the right, we might be able to wedge it behind the table and block the door."

If, if. And, if we did it wrong, brought the bookcase over on us, we'd be in lousier shape than we were already.

Our hands and feet were tied separately then a cord looped from our wrists to a central post, giving us several feet of leeway. We stretched out full-length. It hurt my back so much I wondered how Jimmy bore it. I studied his face then looked quickly away.

Stretched out, our hands above our heads, our feet easily reached the bookcase.

We tugged at it, gingerly at first, then more vigorously when we realized it was well balanced. Slowly, our backs aflame, Jimmy's face a sickly white, we cupped our feet around the legs of the bookcase and pulled and teased it closer to us, then more to the right.

All the while, we could hear the soft slithery crackle of falling mortar, the occasional thunk as a chunk dropped free, the beautiful sounds of rescue.

"Okay," Jimmy grunted. He rested for a moment. I left the final heave to him. He half-rolled onto his side, swung his feet together and shoved the bookcase so that it toppled at an angle. Sweet success. It thudded heavily into the space between the table and the wall, as nice a barricade as one could wish. Any push from outside would only jam it tighter against the table.

They might never get into this damn cellar again. Slowly but surely our friends were coming. But it takes a while to remove a part of a brick wall. A long while. Nine-thirty. Ten. Ten-thirty. Eleven.

Finally the mortar was poked out all around the space of the door and we could hear the murmur of voices. Buddy Wu's voice carried best, an excited nonstop exhortation. A rope slithered over the door-shaped stand of bricks, dropped halfway down and was pulled taut.

"Out of the way," Buddy ordered. "Stand clear there. Okay, one, two, three, let's all pull together . . ."

The stand of bricks teetered, wavered unsteadily for a long moment then, abruptly, it toppled, crashing thunderously away from us. Dust swirled, masking the opening, then Dan plunged through the curtain of dust, moving like a fighter, ready for anything.

Then he saw us.

"Ellen!" And I knew he hadn't expected to see me, that he didn't know I'd been grabbed. He looked from me to Jimmy. "What the hell's going on!"

He had dropped down to untie me before he saw my back. Then, Jimmy's. Dan's face turned a dull angry red and the words came in a soft almost unintelligible rush. I reached out and grabbed his hand when he turned toward the doorway we had blocked. It took Jimmy and Buddy and me to stop him.

"All right," he said finally, "all right." He took a deep breath, then, his face still angry, he untied me and Jimmy. Miss Chow helped me to my feet.

"Get the cops, Buddy," Dan ordered. "Hurry."

Buddy was turning to go back through the uneven opening into his cellar storeroom when Jimmy said sharply, "Wait, Buddy! Wait!" Jimmy looked nervously toward the blocked door to the hallway. "Listen, they may come any time. Everybody stop and listen to me!" The urgency in his voice held us, turned every face toward him.

"Miss Chow," he called her to him and his voice was gentle. "Miss Chow, did you give the fossils to them?"

There wasn't much hope in Jimmy's voice, but, still, a dream dies hard.

"I looked at your note very carefully," she said, "and I felt that it was genuine."

Jimmy sighed, nodded. "I know, and nobody could possibly blame you . . ."

"But I did not feel," she interrupted, "that the young man who gave me the note had a good heart." She shook her head back and forth. "When I gave the skull to you, agreed to have you sell the fossils to have money enough to save the hotel, I only did so because I trusted you." She looked solemnly at Jimmy.

He nodded again but slowly, listening hard.

"I did not trust this young man, this Ted."

I swear no one breathed. It was that quiet in the dusty dim cellar.

"You were right not to trust him," Jimmy said bitterly. "But, I had to tell them where the fossils were because they stopped beating on me and were starting in on Dr Christie. God, I'm sorry, Miss Chow. I wrote the note because I was afraid they would hurt you if you didn't let them have the bones." He stared at her. "You did give them the bones. Didn't you?"

"Oh, no," she said simply.

"But how in the world . . ."

Miss Chow smiled, a serene confident smile. "That was quite easy, Jimmy. I merely told them a truth and a lie."

"The truth?" Buddy asked.

"I told Ted that I no longer had the bones. Of course, they searched my room, but, as you know, that was a simple matter and it convinced them I was telling the truth."

"The lie?" Dan asked.

She looked a little shamefaced. "I do hope you will forgive me and I'm so glad I was able to call you at your office and bring us together to try and find Jimmy, but it was the first thing that came to my mind and you are, after all, such a big young man, I felt sure they would have a difficult time attacking you, and it has, I'm happy to say, worked out all for the best."

Dan laughed softly. "So you told them big brother had the bones, huh?"

Reluctantly, she nodded.

"That's all right. But I'm glad, too, that you called me before they got to me. As a matter of fact, it must have been close. I remember now that as I stepped out of the elevator at my office, I saw two young guys getting on the up-elevator. It may have been our friends going up to pay me a call."

"I knew, of course, that I had to follow them after I told them you had the fossils," Miss Chow said quickly. "I did so and they never even looked back! I suppose they thought there was nothing to fear from an old lady. I followed them directly to the Middle Kingdom Gallery and then I felt sure I knew what had happened. When they went inside, I called you from a pay telephone. And you knew enough of what had happened to agree with me that Jimmy must be a captive at the Gallery."

The door to the hall didn't move more than a half-inch before it stubbed into the wedged bookcase so that didn't make a lot of noise. It was the sharp exclamation of surprise from beyond the door that jerked our heads around and set us into a furious flurry of motion.

Dan simply bent down and lifted Jimmy to his feet and ran for the irregular opening. Buddy took Miss Chow's arm and mine and we were right behind them.

Behind us, we heard the hard regular thump and they thudded against the door, trying to push it in, but they succeeded only in shoving the bookcase tighter against the heavy rosewood table.

In the next cellar, Dan stopped abruptly. "What the hell are we running for?" he demanded. "Like I said before, let's call the cops. It's a matter of two kidnappings and torture. Let's stop playing games with these bastards."

Jimmy held onto his brother's arm for support and I saw, with horror, that blood was dripping slowly onto the floor from the opened wounds on his back. But he ignored it, crying, "No, Dan! There isn't time. And none of it matters if we can save the Green Door. We'll see about it later, but right now time's running out.

"I've got it all set up!" Jimmy said desperately. "At seven-thirty tonight. Behind the pillars at Grant and Bush. The fossils for one hundred and fifty grand and that's enough to buy the Green Door. Don't you see, Dan, we don't have time to call the cops! My God, it would take hours to get it all straight." He looked down at his watch. "It's almost noon now."

He moved away from Dan, walked unsteadily toward Miss Chow. "Because I'm right, aren't I? You know where the fossils are. We haven't lost them. We can still save the Green Door, can't we?"

Buddy and I, our ears hanging out to hear, were busy dragging a heavy banquet table to block the hole between the cellars.

"So who can complain if part of the wall just collapses into my storeroom?" Buddy murmured.

I grinned at him. Sweat trickled down his face, his dark suit was rumpled and dusty, his hands scratched and bruised, and I could have hugged every plump, out-of-shape inch of him.

We had the table upended, covering the opening, and four more tables stacked vertically to jam the covering table before we heard the first splintery sound of breaking wood from the cellar beyond.

And we had listened as Miss Chow described her uncertainty about what to do with the fossils after Dan and I visited her. She wasn't fooled by our visit even though, she said with a little smile and nod, she found us very charming. She knew we didn't have Jimmy's confidence or we would have spoken frankly to her about Peking Man. So she made her decision: she must hide the fossils.

Buddy and I heard the screech of wood in the cellar beyond. "Hey folks, I'm hanging on every word, but let's go upstairs to my office for the finale. There's some riffraff at the door."

It would still take them a minute or so to reach our makeshift barrier. There was no knowing whether they would try to breach it. But there was no point in waiting around to see.

We went up a narrow backstair that opened into the hall outside Buddy's office. He left us briefly and came back with Joe, a huge young man who made Buddy and Dan look small. I suppose even the nicest restaurants have someone at hand for emergencies. I didn't worry about an attack from the cellar after I saw Joe. He listened closely to Buddy's instructions, his mouth drawn up in a perennial smile from the half-moon scar that pulled the skin on his right cheek.

"I always believe in securing my rear," Buddy observed as he shepherded us into his office. Once settled, we all looked at Miss Chow, who had decided she must hide the fossils.

"In your room . . ." Dan began doubtfully.

"Oh no," she said quickly. "I knew that my room offered no safety to Peking Man. And that proved to be true for that young man did search my room. Of course, the fossils were gone by then."

"But where?" Jimmy demanded, almost ferociously.

So she told us. After Dan and I left, she opened the metal container in which she had carried the bones (U.S. Customs wasn't concerned, after all, for many Chinese venerate their dead and, for many years, bones were sent home to China for burial so what was odd about an old lady from China bringing along the bones of her ancestors?), and lifted out the yellowed hard fossils and dumped all of them into a cardboard suitcase. She wedged the suitcase into her sturdy knitting bag, and, after a little thought, added her sewing kit with its variety of needles, thread and scissors.

It had taken her almost an hour to walk the six long blocks from the hotel to Market Street, but then it was easy. A nickel for the streetcar, a swift ride to Polk, and only three blocks to go.

There was a moment of stunned silence after she finished

and everyone realized where the bones were hidden.

It was Jimmy who summed it up.

"My God, what are we going to do?"

EIGHTEEN

"It would be easier to get into a nunnery on Saturday afternoon," Buddy offered.

Miss Chow was distressed.

"Oh, that never occurred to me. But it was the only place outside of Chinatown that I had visited in recent years." She looked at Jimmy imploringly. "You remember when the busloads of us attended the city council meetings to ask for more housing for the elderly."

"Yeah," Jimmy said limply. "The second floor?"

She nodded unhappily. "I don't suppose," she began in a small voice, "there is anyone we could call, anyone who would open the building for us . . ."

Four heads shook back and forth. Open City Hall? On a Saturday afternoon? Maybe for the millenium. Not much short of it. Certainly not for our ill-assorted little group of conspirators.

"So your buyer's set to show up at Bush and Grant at seven-thirty?" Dan asked.

Jimmy nodded.

We all looked at our watches. Fifteen minutes past noon.

"Can you get in touch with him, reschedule . . ."

Jimmy shook his head. "No way. Even if I could, it would probably blow the deal. He's skittish anyway. I talked to him on the phone this morning and he damn near whispered the whole time and he has a funny accent . . ."

"Who is he?" I asked. Maybe it was a curator, an anthropologist, somebody who would take care of the bones, then I could be excused for not blowing the whistle.

"I'm not sure," Jimmy said uncertainly. "But he has to be okay even though he didn't sound like the guy I set it up with."

Jimmy hadn't fooled around. "I called the Chinese Embassy in Ottawa and asked to be connected with someone who had the authority to discuss the return of Peking Man."

Simple. Direct. And, apparently, successful.

"It seemed like forever before anybody came on the line." He suddenly looked very young. "You see, I was paying for the call and you can imagine how it was mounting up. But there'll be enough money—if we can get to the bones. Anyway, this old guy finally came on the line and we talked, oh, it must have been for half-an-hour. The funny thing is, I don't think he ever doubted that I had the real thing. I guess there's something about telling somebody the truth. I mean, I didn't tell him my name or Miss Chow's but I told him how Dr Tang got the bones and how a friend brought them to the United States and kept them all these years and how we needed a certain amount of money, not even nearly as much as the fossils were worth, but we would let them go for a hundred and fifty thousand, and I told him what the skull looked like that I had . . ."

"Where is it?" I interrupted sharply. I had forgotten all about that first skull. But, if Jimmy had not told about Miss Chow until he protected me, then more than likely he hadn't revealed where he had hidden that skull, either.

"It's okay. I left it at my friend's in Berkeley. See, I was on my way to Miss Chow's to get the rest of the fossils when those thugs got me. Anyway, I told the old guy at the Embassy about the funny kind of dent on the right side of the skull and he got real excited and said he knew which skull I meant because Dr Weidenreich had shown that particular skull to him in 1939. It seems he knew Weidenreich even though he wasn't a scientist himself. So we set it up for him to come to San Francisco and call me this morning."

The phone-call came right on schedule but the talk wasn't easy then. The man whispered and kept turning down all Jimmy's suggestions on where to meet.

"He kept saying he wanted to be where there were lots of people. I told him this was the right night to be in San Francisco, nothing but people and all of them packed into Chinatown for the big parade. He liked that fine." Jimmy frowned. "He sure acted spooky. I'd almost think it wasn't the guy I talked to before but it had to be because he mentioned that skull again and he had my phone number and knew the password we'd worked out."

Password.

I won't say I had a premonition. Nothing that specific. It was just a flicker of distress, the clear sharp knowledge that Jimmy had plunged into a world much darker and more dangerous than a make-believe game of passwords could ever be.

But that tremor at the incongruity of passwords was lost in a flood of relief that Jimmy had at least set up an exchange with responsible people. If the sale went through, the fossils would be going home to China and nobody could quarrel with that.

Although, if the story ever became public and I was linked to it, I could already hear the carping, "Dr Christie, as a responsible member of the scientific community, surely you made every effort . . ."

Dan was shaking his head. ". . . no way, Jimmy. How the hell could we get in? You can't just smash a window at City Hall and climb in. There would be a patrol car there in seconds! And the damn thing's lit up at night, even if we could wait 'til after dark. I don't see any way."

"Alfred," Buddy said excitedly.

Dan and Jimmy, Miss Chow and I all looked at him.

"Alfred," he repeated loudly.

"Oh," Dan said slowly, "you mean your brother, Alfred, the one who . . ."

"Right. He'll help us. Sure he will."

Once Buddy made the plan clear to us, we all chimed in and, in five minutes, we had come up with the damnedest scheme. Only in California, I thought. And an idea that would occur only to a Californian.

Once Buddy had a plan, he wasn't content merely to run with it. He led the charge.

But first, he found a clean chef's coat from his kitchen, gently hung it around Jimmy's shoulders, then packed him off to see another Wu brother, Calvin, a general practitioner who would treat an unusual wound and keep his mouth shut.

Jimmy didn't want to go.

"You want maybe to collapse from loss of blood? Besides, you are staining my office floor. Look, Calvin will fix you up and then you might as well get some rest because, if everything works out and we get the bones, you'll be a busy man tonight."

Miss Chow would not be detached. I didn't blame her. She intended to be in on the finale of the fossils that had been in her charge for so many years.

Me, I was to go along to Calvin's, get my back treated then rejoin the troupe and become part of the dramatic personae along with Dan.

Buddy, of course, was producer and director.

It was a gem of a plan but we were almost undone before we had begun by something absolutely beyond our control—the weather.

That morning, a million years ago, had dawned clear and

lovely, the sky a clean-washed blue, the air whippy and fresh, Dan said. But, when we came out of the East Wind Restaurant, San Francisco had turned her face to the hills, the sunshine gone. Low soft rainsodden clouds hung heavily in the sky and Grant Avenue looked older, colder.

"If it rains . . ." Buddy muttered.

He didn't have to finish. If it rained, everything was kaput.

Alfred was waiting for us, his truck parked in a no-parking zone right in front of City Hall, a huge domed building that looks enough like the Capitol in Washington to be its double. Alfred was Buddy twenty pounds heavier, five years older, emanating the same confidence, the same élan.

For the first time, I began to believe in our wild venture, and, for the first time that tumultuous day, felt the unhappy certainty that I must make a choice. And every foot I walked with them, every word I didn't say, would make that choice more difficult.

But there was no chance now of a quiet word with Dan. No chance to justify myself. No chance to ask him to consider my feelings.

You can change your mind at the amusement park up to the time you climb into the roller coaster car and it clanks up the wooden rails, reaches the top, then begins to hurtle down. Then there's no more time.

Everything was moving fast now, the car hurtling down the steep roller coaster incline. Alfred and three young assistants were rolling the pedal-powered dolly down the ramp from the truck, wheeling it to the south side of the portico, fastening the tripod legs, mounting the camera on the head, checking the light meter, unloading three tripod-mounted lamps.

Dan looked dashing in his ill-fitting khaki tunic, jodhpurs and a cap that sported a small rounded black bill. He tried to help unload, too, until Buddy hissed at him that actors are unionized, dummy, and they don't carry the cameras.

Dan and I stood in the shadow of the south wall of the City Hall portico along with Miss Chow, whose bright black eyes sparkled with excitement, while Alfred's assistants unfolded and set up an aluminum ladder. One of the boys ran lightly up the metal steps to the second-floor balcony and hung the rope ladder, jerking at it to make sure it was secure.

Then Buddy was calling out, "Okay, Ellen, up you go."

And my last chance to speak out to Dan was gone.

It had been my decision, my insistence, that I be the one to go up. I had pointed out that in Arkansas breaking and entering was a felony and any lawyer convicted of a felony would be disbarred. I didn't know the penalty in California—a felony, Dan agreed—but I knew damn well that any lawyer caught breaking into City Hall was in trouble.

Nobody could disbar an anthropologist.

An anthropologist could be fired, Dan pointed out.

But I was stubborn and Dan, admittedly, had a lot more to lose. It made sense. So now Buddy waited for me to start up the ladder.

The Great Break-In.

"You shouldn't have a bit of trouble, dear," Miss Chow whispered encouragingly.

No, I didn't think I would have any trouble, but it was hard to start climbing, anyway. The grey sky, the cold wet air—and the police car pulling up at the kerb.

I gingerly straightened the brown knapsack on my shoulders, it pressed a little uncomfortably against the bandages under my jacket, and started up the ladder, awkward in dark blue baggy trousers and a padded Mao jacket. Buddy's voice carried clearly even after I clambered over the parapet onto the balcony.

"Hello, Officer, how are you today? We're hoping to finish up this scene before it rains. Second time we've shot here and we had to wait for all these damn sunny days to pass, storyline needs clouds . . ."

The policeman murmured a question and Buddy swept right on and I could hear snatches of it ". . . Athena Productions . . . my cameraman, Alfred Wu . . . great story, see, this Manchurian general and a Russian woman agent . . . side of City Hall looks exactly like this building on T'ien An Men Square in Peking . . . okay, get those spots in place . . . move the boom this way . . . you'll excuse me, Officer . . ."

The parapet was tall enough to hide me as I knelt near a window in the shadow of one of the thick pillars that supported the French Renaissance roof. The knapsack lay in front of me, open and with several tools spread out that the officer would have found very interesting.

A physical anthropologist must achieve mastery of a number of diverse tools and many sophisticated techniques, so I had a fairly wide acquaintance with lots of gadgets, but I'd never used glasscutters before.

I slipped on the protective goggles, put on soft leather gloves and held the battery-powered cutter to the glass.

Buddy's voice, easy, friendly, relaxed, drifted up to me.

Why didn't that dammed policeman go away?

It was a huge window. I didn't try to figure out how it was locked or even whether it was locked for I knew it would not have been opened in so many years that it would be stuck tighter than the Salvation Army to a kettle. I was on my knees for the windowsill was only two feet above the roof. I pushed the button on the cutter and held the blade to the glass then, in a panic, turned it off. Its sharp nasal whine shocked me and I was sure there would be shouts of alarm from below.

Nothing but Buddy's ebullient voice, "Come back and see

us again, Officer. It's always a pleasure . . ."

I took a deep breath, switched on the cutter and, running it from right to left, sliced a two-foot-long horizontal line, then turned the cutter down for a foot and a half.

I stopped again, took another deep breath, and pulled the fist-sized suction cup from the knapsack. Pushing it firmly in the centre of my square and keeping a firm grip on it, I switched on the cutter, sliced the bottom horizontal line then turned up for the final vertical cut.

The rectangle of glass lifted neatly out. I laid it carefully on the balcony, well out of my way, then loosened the suction cup and dropped it back into the knapsack.

I lifted out a small quilted pad, spread it on the sharp lower edge of my entryway, then leaned inside. Dark and empty halls stretched to my right and left. I listened for a moment, then dropped the knapsack inside. Behind me and below, I could hear Buddy, still having a high old time, in-structing Dan, "Stop right there, yeah, halfway up, look back over your shoulder; My God, you hear troops coming, that's right, shock and dismay, okay, cameras ready . . ."

I climbed through the hole in the window carefully, very carefully. Two feet of knifesharp glass, even under cover of a quilted pad, had my close attention. Once inside, I scooped up the knapsack, turned to my right and ran softly up the wide marble-floored hallway. It looked and smelled like any public building anywhere. I passed the closed doors to a courtroom and wondered if that was where Miss Chow's meeting had been held. I was picturing Miss Chow and a long line of little old ladies, round hopeful faces, clasped hands, slacks and soft slippers, picturing them and wondering at their thoughts that day so the sudden sharp sound was even more unexpected and shocking.

I stopped, lifted my head and listened. It was such a simple homely sound to drag the breath from my lungs, set my heart to pounding. The click of a closing door. But I had no business here. There was no tale I could spin that would explain my presence in this darkened hallway.

If a door closes, someone has gone in or out. I listened for footsteps and looked frantically about for a hiding place. The hallway stretched up and down, stark, bare, empty. No place to hide.

The thick quilted Mao jacket was hot. Sweat beaded my face, slid down my back.

Nothing happened. It was utterly still, no footsteps, no voices, nothing but the quick sound of my breath and, far away, distant as a train whistle in the night, the faint chatter of Buddy, directing his troupe.

They were waiting for me. Every instant that I hesitated increased their risk and mine. That policeman might wonder, might check to see if a movie company did have permission to film outside City Hall. So, one feather-light footfall after another, I tiptoed on up the hall, fearing each instant that a door would open, signalling the end of my charade.

But wasn't that, I realized suddenly, what I wanted to happen? Wouldn't that give me the easiest out of all? If I were caught, who could blame me? Then I could see that my museum director was called and the FBI. Peking Man would be recovered with no more chance of loss or damage.

I passed closed and darkened doors their legends inscribed on frosted glass, Public Utilities Commission, Purchaser of Supplies.

At the end of the hall, I stopped, looked to my left down another long hall and saw the bright white square of light shining through the frosted glass of the Mayor's Office of Economic Development. Directly across the hall was my goal, Room 279 with its modest inscription, WOMEN.

Someone worked overtime behind that lighted door. Some diligent public servant. I could tap on the door and Peking Man would be found—and forever lost to Jimmy and Miss Chow. There wouldn't be a sale at 7.30 pm to start the fossils off into an uncertain future.

Peking Man would be safe—if I knocked on the door.

But I didn't have the fossils in hand yet.

Still tiptoeing, I moved quietly up the hall to Room 279. It, too, was an old-fashioned door with a frosted glass panel. I turned the knob, stepped inside and softly closed the door after me.

I stood in a small rectangular anteroom. It opened into the washroom with lavatories on the left wall, the toilet cubicles on the right. Just to the left of me, in the anteroom was a dusty worn sofa, its back cushions missing, its two maroon seat cushions lumpy and misshapen.

Again I had trouble breathing. But, this time, it wasn't fear. It was the same breathless excitement that marks the beginnings of any step into the unknown.

One hurried step and I was beside the sofa. I slipped the knapsack off my back, rested it on the cold marble floor. It was dusky in the anteroom, the only light coming through windows in the washroom that opened onto an airshaft.

I pulled out a portable flashlight, sat it on its base, switched it on. The light was aimed at the sofa and my body was between the flash and the door to the hall. It shouldn't show a bit.

Then, quickly, quickly, I pulled out the scissors. It was easy to find her neat professional stitches and I could hear her gentle voice telling me so earnestly, "You see, I almost never leave Chinatown, but, when I knew I must hide Peking Man, I felt very desperate for a hiding place. I go to so few places, my sewing factory, the hospital, Portsmouth Square. And then I thought of the time we went to City Hall to ask for more housing. Oh, there must have been seventy-five or a hundred of us! Everyone treated us so nicely and, while I was there, I did need to use the restroom and I remembered the sofa, such a, well it isn't kind to say of government property, but such a shabby worn wreck of an old couch and I thought then that if anybody would just take a needle to it, it would look better; the cushions ripped, you know, and then I thought it would be such a good place to put the bones for who would ever think of looking inside one of those old lumpy maroon cushions?"

Nobody, but nobody, I crooned to myself, as I snipped along that firm line of stitching.

The entire staff of the Mayor's Office of Economic Development could have entered the restroom en masse and I wouldn't have noticed because my fingers were poking inside the opened seam and I felt cardboard.

The shabby cardboard suitcase was wedged inside. I tugged and strained and pulled it out. It wasn't locked. The lock was broken. I lifted the lid, rustled through the wadded up newsprint used as padding, and then, in the dim light of a flashlight, kneeling on the scuffed floor of a public restroom, I looked at the most incredible collection of fossils ever salvaged from man's early days.

Two skulls and there, yes, a piece of jaw, half a femur, a muslin bag filled with teeth. It was the most complete skull that caught my gaze, drew my fingers. I held it close to my face, so close, the empty eye sockets level with my eyes.

You stood on a windswept hill, I thought, hurried down faintly seen trails, knelt to make fire, you prayed and loved and laughed; you are a part of me and all the millions of men everywhere, you are from our beginnings and you are here now, this instant; my fingers feel your bone, know your reality.

I don't know how long it was before I stood, a little stiffly, replaced the fossils, smoothed down the crumpled newspapers, shut the suitcase and crammed it into the knapsack. Then the scissors and, switching it off, the flashlight.

I opened the door to the hallway. Nothing had changed. Light still shone through the frosted glass panel of the office across the hall.

I took one step, two, nearer that door, my hand outstretched. There wasn't any question, really, about what I should do.

Peking Man was irreplaceable. He had been lost once, hidden for more than a quarter of a century. Five steps more, the turning of a knob and Peking Man would be safe forever.

I closed my eyes, then, heartsick, opened them and took another step.

Outside, daring jail and embarrassment, Dan and Buddy waited. Dan must be tired now, clinging to that awkward rope-ladder, and even Buddy must be flagging, trying to keep up the presence. And Alfred, who was good enough to bring his crew and make it all possible, faced trouble, too.

Now, close to the lighted door panel, I could hear the sound of typing in the room beyond.

Jimmy was waiting for me, too, his swollen lacerated back bandaged now and, surely, something taken to ease the pain. But Jimmy waited to see if the bones would come and the sale go through and the Green Door Hotel be saved.

The Green Door Hotel. Forty-three old people. No, forty-two since Ru'Lan Wong died. No, my mind circled around, forty-three because her room would have been taken by now, refuge for another old and lonely soul.

Old ladies like Emily Chow and old men like the one who gripped the doorframe 'til his hand whitened and asked, though he knew the answer, "Where will we go? What will happen to us?"

Peking Man's safety or their home?

Peking Man's fears had long since been laid to rest, no tears to run down his face. Did it much matter where bones were laid when people had no beds?

My hand touched the cool metal of the knob. Just a twist, a quick decided turn, and the decision would be made.

And, an unattractive voice whispered within, you know that things always come out and—if you take the bones, help put them up for cash—well, the truth will come out someday and, when it does, Ellen Christie, there will go your job and your future.

I loved my work. I was proud of it. Without it, I would be diminished, not quite a person.

A down-at-heels cheap hotel, a city's better off without that sort.

Emily's face and that small, so small figure on the stretcher and old hands clinging to a doorframe.

My hand fell away from the knob, I tightened my grip on the knapsack, turned and ran up the hallway.

Screw my career.

NINETEEN

Life is a series of gambles, little guesses as to how the dice will roll. Will it rain today, shall I carry an umbrella, is the hot dog fresh, shall I walk this way or that?

Sometimes the gambles are for bigger stakes and your hands sweat as you await the roll.

"For God's sake," Jimmy had pled, "don't look at me!"

But he had agreed, reluctantly, that Dan and Miss Chow and Buddy and I could be there, part of the milling hundreds that night in Chinatown, Chinese of all ages, dark-coated old ladies, families, babies in arm, and thousands of whites, students, housewives, tourists, natives, everybody jammed shoulder to shoulder, lining the parade route fifteen deep to watch the most magnificent parade of the year when Chinatown's dragons, symbols of luck and prosperity, wind up and down hilly streets, tossing their massive heads, whipping back and forth their sinuous tails; huge, jaunty, glorious.

Every kerb along the parade route was full by six-thirty. Vendors hawked balloons and boys darted up and down the streets, tossing firecrackers. The rat-a-tat-tat of the exploding firecrackers mingled with the vendors' patter and the restless shuffling surflike noise of thousands of people, talking, moving a little this way and that, waiting, laughing.

Even the rain couldn't ruin this parade. Umbrellas sprouted along the kerbs like varicoloured mushrooms, newspapers were folded and balanced atop heads, caps donned, and nobody went home.

I pulled up the hood on my raincoat and blessed my

fleece-lined apres-ski boots as the rain turned heavier, sweeping in shimmering waves to glisten in the light of the firetruck spotlight that was turned down Grant to light the way for the parade.

Spectators, hunching close for warmth now, spread around the gate to Chinatown, the three-tiered greenglazed tile arch that marks Chinatown's beginnings on Grant. The parade would climb up Grant to the gate then turn east on Bush, not traversing the actual heart of Chinatown for the streets were too narrow and the danger of fire too great.

Jimmy stood beneath the street light just past the gate on the west side of the street. Over the shoulder of his raincoat hung a red leather bota and, in his right hand, he carried a woven straw shopping bag. Enough, certainly, to make his identity sure.

Dan, Miss Chow, Buddy and I each waited on a separate corner so we wouldn't be noticeable as a group, just in case Mr Wilkie Lee's helpful young men were wandering the streets.

This was where I made a little gamble. The street was filling when we first came but we were still early enough to choose our spots and I manoeuvred so that I ended up standing in the cover of the pagoda-like roof on the west side of the gate that spanned Grant. I could, if I turned a little sideways, see back to the lamp post where Jimmy waited.

The light shone down on Jimmy's face.

I was gambling that at some point the man Jimmy was going to meet would stand in the shaft of light from the lamp post. Just for an instant. That was all I would need.

Anthropologists have to be a nosy bunch to find out things their subjects might just as soon not reveal. So, sometimes, it's helpful to make pictures without the giveaway brilliance of a flash. If your camera is good enough and your film is fast enough, all you need is a little light. Just a little, just for an instant.

I had my Nikon, dangling from a strap at my wrist, and it was loaded with Kodak Tri-X film. All I needed was just an instant—and a face beneath a lamp post.

Jimmy would be furious if he knew. But there was no reason why he should ever know. I would watch and, at the right instant, lift my hand, take a picture—or, with the incredibly quick speed of a Nikon, two or three.

I wasn't sure of my motive. I had, in the last three days, done the unexpected, surprised myself so often, that I felt a little like a stranger to myself. I had decided, against my better judgement, against all training and instinct, to let the fossils be bartered away. Now I wanted a picture of the buyer. To put in my scrapbook? But, still, it was something, a tiny link to the fossils; not enough, perhaps, but something.

So we all waited in the rain. I clung to my camera and Jimmy stood in lamplight, holding the woven straw shopping bag.

We heard, first, the rising sound of cheers. The crowd moved restlessly, like penned cattle. Far down the sloping street, a band swung from Market onto Grant. The parade was coming!

I glanced at my watch. Fifteen past seven. It wouldn't be long now. One more time, I looked quickly over my shoulder, but Jimmy still stood alone, no one near him, no one noticing him.

It was a goodnatured rowdy free-tongued crowd. Every time the rain grew heavier, some few along the kerb would open and raise umbrellas and the cry would go up, "Down with the umbrellas, down in front so everybody can see, hey, what's the matter with a little rain," and, slowly, one by one, all the umbrellas would be drawn down except for one flamboyant white one decorated with orange flowers. It only waved a little higher.

"For shame," a voice cried above me and I looked up to see a bearded youth perched precariously on the concrete crossbar that ran beneath the pagoda roof. Rain spattered on his face, but he was grinning. "Hey, white umbrella," he yelled, "don't be such a turkey," but the umbrella stayed high. He looked down, saw me watching, and laughed aloud, "Hey, isn't this fun!"

I smiled back, enjoying his good humour. "Be careful," I offered, "that looks a little slippery."

"It's the best view in Chinatown. Those five-dollar bleacher seats on Kearney can't touch it."

Then a murmur ran through the crowd, a high-rising swell of excitement, for the first dragon had turned from Market onto Grant and was beginning to writhe and curve up the hill, the lights along its spine bobbing and weaving as the boys beneath it ran from side to side up the street.

Caught up in the colour and excitement, I almost forgot to check behind me and, when I did, it was with the feeling of having missed something because what I saw was wrong, all wrong!

Jimmy, his face wary and uncertain, was listening intently to a man, who kept jerking his head toward the shadows of an awning. Finally, Jimmy nodded and turned to move the few steps into the darkness where I could scarcely see them. But I knew this couldn't be the man from the Chinese Embassy in Ottawa. It wasn't possible. The man wasn't Chinese!

He and Jimmy were only dim shapes in the shadow of the awning, but I had seen the man clearly. He stood just over medium height. He wore a heavy winter suit of dull grey. His face was blunt, high coloured, heavy jowled, and he wore a bristly blond beard.

A brass band preceded the dragon and it was swinging past us now, blaring out, oddly, *Amazing Grace*. Firecrackers sputtered and popped in the street behind us, raining down from fire escapes and rooftops.

Still I twisted to see behind me. It couldn't be the right man! Surely Jimmy would be careful. He knew we were here, ready to help him, if need be.

Jimmy, the straw carry-all still firmly in his left hand, moved back near the lamp post and propped an attache case on top of a parking meter. He opened it, bent close, reached inside. A loping band of teenagers ran down the sidewalk toward him. He looked up and quickly slammed the attache case shut. He turned and moved back into the shadowy alcove. There was a flurry of movement then the other man, clutching the straw bag, darted down the sidewalk toward me, pushing into the thick of the crowd massed at the corner.

I held the Nikon shoulder high, ready, then it was this instant or never as he shoved his way into the crowd and was even with me, only four feet away.

One picture, two, three, the fourth caught the back of his head.

The light wasn't quite as bright as beneath the lamp post but there was an almost daylight-sheen cast by the fire truck spotlight and light spilled from a hot dog stand at the corner. Enough, there should have been enough.

He was slipping free of the crush at the corner when someone threw a firecracker and it exploded by his right foot. Panicked, he swung around to look back toward Jimmy and he shouted in a language I didn't know.

Then, from above me, the friendly boy called out, speaking also in that language that I didn't know. The man looked up, colour spread back into his face, he nodded and, abruptly, he turned and began to run heavily, skirting the fire truck, crossing Bush and heading down Grant. He was almost immediately swallowed up in the shifting moving crowd.

I looked up, the boy was cheering now because the dragon had reached the top of the hill, was weaving and bobbing, its fantastic face, painted with swirls of red and gold, nodding to the spectators.

I waited until the dragon was past and a high school band marching by, then I called up, "What did you say to him?"

The boy looked down, puzzled. "Huh?"

"To the man who shouted. What did you say?"

"Oh, I told him not to worry, that it was just firecrackers."

Another dragon was turning the corner, far away, down at the base of Grant and the crowd began to murmur, the sound swelling and rising.

"What language did he speak?"

"Russian."

He misread my expression.

"You'd be surprised," he continued from his damp aerial perch, "how many people speak Russian in San Francisco. It's my major and I'm always getting a chance to practice it. Anyway, you can find people here who speak all kinds of languages, it's . . ."

I didn't really listen to the rest of his likable chatter.

Russian. Indeed, I was surprised.

TWENTY

The big rip-off.

Of course, nobody should have been surprised. The Babylonians and the Elamites knew about thieves' honour.

"It looked like it was all there!" Jimmy said furiously.

Stacks of twenty-dollar bills were tumbled onto the middle of the conference table in Dan's office. Lots of stacks. Six hundred and twenty-five stacks in all but only about twenty of them were made up of twenty-dollar bills all the way down. The rest had a twenty on the top and bottom and ones in between.

Miss Chow and I added them up. It was a respectable total. Seventy-eight thousand eight hundred and fifty dollars. But it was forty-six thousand one hundred and fifty dollars short of the going price for the Green Door Hotel.

And there wasn't a dammed thing we could do about it.

If we had been real crooks, we could have put out a call, tried to track the man down. But we were one social worker, one lawyer, one little old lady, one restaurant owner and one anthropologist. Not much muscle there.

Dan was the only one who showed any interest in my photography. Jimmy just shrugged. Even I couldn't see much use for it. I only knew that my first instinct, to block the sale, had been right. I was culpable. Damn culpable.

"What gets me," Jimmy exploded, "is that I was such a chump! I should have known it was all wrong when he wasn't Chinese."

"He was Russian," I announced.

Four faces looked at me seriously.

"ESP?" Dan asked.

So I told them of the cheerful college student and the fire-crackers.

"Russian," Dan repeated thoughtfully. Dan reminded us that China and Russia share the world's longest border and great mutual mistrust. It didn't take too much savvy to know that Chinese embassies everywhere were likely objects of curiosity to Russian agents. If a Russian agent in Ottawa was monitoring telephone conversations at the Embassy on Friday and if that agent were both greedy and daring . . .

We all nodded solemnly. Everybody could see how it might have happened. But that was no comfort at all to Jimmy.

He pounded the conference table and the stacks of money slithered and jumped on its polished surface. "This isn't enough! Now there isn't any way we can save the Green Door!"

I almost spoke up, then I closed my mouth firmly again. I know how a lawyer's mind works. They have such a finicky attitude toward what you can do and what you can't do. An anthropologist is more interested in the art of the possible. So, I kept my mouth shut.

Instead, I sighed wearily, yawned, said I was sorry that everything hadn't worked out, but that I believed I would go home now.

Dan immediately got up and began to reach for my coat and scarf. "I'll see Ellen and Miss Chow home, Jimmy. They're about done in. Besides, there isn't anything more we can do, anyway."

Everyone began to mill around. Buddy said he would be glad to take Miss Chow home. I stepped closer to Jimmy, put my hands on his arms, bent close as if to kiss his cheek, but I whispered softly, "Call me later. I have an idea," then I touched his cheek softly with my lips. "Some money's better than none," I said aloud.

It was close to eleven when Dan walked me up the stairs to my apartment. I handed him my key and he opened the door. I wanted to ask him in and I knew he wanted to come in. But Jimmy would be calling.

We stood in the doorway. Slowly, he reached out, pulled me close to him. He didn't say anything. He didn't have to. I lifted my face to his and his mouth came down on mine and I didn't care if the phone rang forever.

It was Dan who said indistinctly, "Your phone . . ."

"Yes." Then, quickly, "Oh yes, I'd better . . ."

"Tomorrow," he said. "I'll see you tomorrow."

I was smiling when I reached down to answer the telephone. It was Jimmy. I told him my scheme. He was silent for a long moment then he laughed and his laugh reminded me of Dan, an open infectious boisterous laugh.

"By God, Ellen, you're all right." Jimmy laughed again. "Dan won't like it."

"I don't suggest we mention it to him."

That tickled him, too. "At least, not for now, huh?"

I set my alarm for early. It was going to be a full day. I started off in my darkroom at seven. I wore rubber gloves as I developed the film. I kept on the rubber gloves while I picked out some contact paper from the middle of the stack where I would not have touched it. I had several plans for the upcoming photographs but putting my fingerprints on them wasn't included.

The prints were first-rate, clear, sharp, distinct. My Russian, as I thought of him, couldn't have come across better if he had posed. The camera had caught him full face, high forehead, thick grey hair receding from a widow's peak, a blunt nose, pouchy jowls, bristly grey-blond beard and there, just visible above the beard on his left cheek, the jagged tip of a scar that likely ran down the full cheek.

Oh baby, I thought, anybody who ever knew you will recognize this picture. We're going to teach you not to be such a greedy bastard.

Dan called at eight and I wondered whether he just assumed I was an early riser.

I asked him. He laughed, softly this time. "If you aren't, you will be," he declared. "I always get up early."

There was a good lot of talk along that line, fun for us, not particularly of interest to anyone else.

"How about Fisherman's Wharf for lunch?"

Damn, I wanted to. Wanted to. But today was duty day.

"Dan, I missed work Friday, you know, and there is a project I have to work on . . ."

I could sense his surprise, his sudden uncertainty, and I hurried to add, ". . . not that I wanted to. But you know how it is. So, please, can you come for dinner tomorrow night?"

That would be Monday night and it would all be done, success or failure, by Monday night.

"Tomorrow night?"

"Yes."

"I want to see you before then."

"I . . ." Damn, I would hurry, get it done. "I want to see you, too. Tonight then. At eight."

A busy, busy day.

Jimmy called at mid morning, told me he had the contract ready, had talked to Miss Chow and had I read the Sunday newspaper?

I said no and rustled through the sections to find the story, just a small insignificant story on an inside page about the odd episode in Ottawa when a member of the Chinese Embassy staff was robbed at the airport parking lot of an attache case by a masked gunman. The Embassy official had declined to confirm the report or reveal what was carried in the case.

When the pictures were finished, two prints of the best shot, I put them in my briefcase. I filed the negatives under R for Russian with no other notation.

Next I took a quick run to the drugstore, and, wearing leather gloves now, I bought the cheapest typing paper and a package of manila envelopes. On to Berkeley and the University library where I rented a carrel with a typewriter. It didn't take long. I put one photo in an envelope addressed to the FBI with the typed information that the subject of the picture had taken possession of the famed Peking Man bones in San Francisco on Saturday, that he would likely attempt to smuggle them out of the United States and that he was believed to be a minor member of the Russian Embassy staff in Ottawa. The second photo went in an envelope addressed to the Chinese Embassy in Ottawa with the same information. I dropped both envelopes into a mail box at the Student Union.

I thought both recipients would find the enclosures interesting.

It was mid-afternoon by the time I got home from Berkeley. I made coffee, straightened the apartment, but, finally, I could put it off no longer.

For several months now, as a regular thing, Richard and I went out for dinner on Monday evenings, usually to Mario's, an inexpensive Italian restaurant not far off Broadway. Richard would drop by my office, wait as I finished up, then we would go out to the parking lot, his car would follow mine home then, in his Fiat, we would drive on to dinner.

No big deal. But a regular thing, an expected end to Mondays. But not this Monday for Dan would be coming to dinner.

Oh, it's hard to do some things.

I dialled and Richard answered. He was stiff at first. "I came last night. But you weren't home."

I told him I was sorry, that it had been . . . unavoidable. Before he could say more, I forced myself to go on.

"Richard, I'm sorry but I won't be able to go out to dinner with you tomorrow night. I'm having dinner . . . with someone else."

The sudden silence told me more than I wanted to know, told me he cared and I wondered with an empty feeling if I had made a hideous mistake. I had known Richard for half-a-year and we had laughed together, enjoyed each other, moved toward love. I had known Dan Lee for half-a-week and not quite that.

Richard cleared his throat, said almost briskly, almost but not quite, "Right, Ellen. I'm . . . sorry you can't make it." He paused, then said quickly, "It was good of you to call."

Good of me to call. Oh, Lord.

"Richard," and it was my voice that broke, "Richard, I'm sorry . . ."

"Oh, that's all right, Ellen. Things . . . happen."

When the call was done, I knew it was the right thing. But that didn't make it a happy thing.

When Dan came at eight, I told him as he stepped in the front door that we weren't going to talk about Peking Man, not once.

"That's okay with me," he said agreeably.

But, of course, I had more than one reason for my ban. I might keep some things from Dan but I wasn't going to tell him any outright lies. And, if we didn't talk about any of it, then, later, he couldn't be too unhappy at my lack of revelations. I hoped. But, really, I don't think we would have talked about Peking Man in any event. Dan's interests lay elsewhere. And so did mine.

When I awoke Monday I wondered if I would be scared. But, oddly, I wasn't. I called the museum, said I had an appointment and would be late to work. I waited until almost ten then walked over to Hyde and took the cable car. I clung to a bar and stood on the outside, welcoming the sharpness of the air, loving San Francisco. I transferred at California and rode down to Old St Mary's and hopped off. The only reminder of Saturday night's parade were the shreds of red firecracker paper underfoot.

Pushing through the heavy door of the Middle Kingdom Gallery, I did feel strange when the quiet young woman, just as she had on Friday, stepped through the beaded curtain and asked if she could help me.

I told her that I wished to speak privately with Mr Lee and she led the way to his office. She knocked, opened the door and said, "Mr Lee, a customer to see you." She stepped back to let me pass and so she didn't see the shock on her employer's face when I walked in. I closed the door behind me before he could speak.

I remembered his calm, impervious face when Dan and I talked to him on Friday, when he had lied about seeing Jimmy, lied without a tremor. I liked the sudden sheen of sweat on his face, the jerk of his throat as he swallowed.

I smiled. I suppose women do have an instinct for the jugular. I decided overstepping that fine line between the legal and the illegal was like sipping brandy, easier and a little more intoxicating every time you did it. Shamelessly, I was enjoying myself.

Mr Wilkie Lee was not enjoying himself. He started to speak, stopped. If he ordered me out, he was as good as admitting his complicity in my kidnapping. But, he did not want to talk to me.

"I am sorry, Miss . . . uh . . . Miss, but I am very busy this morning so you must please be so kind . . ."

"I see no reason to be the least bit kind to you, Mr Lee."

He drew his breath in sharply. His eyes flickered down and I remembered what Jimmy said about the buzzer beneath his desk.

"It won't do you any good to push that buzzer either."

His hand jumped back as if the desk had snapped at him.

"I have friends waiting," I continued smoothly. "To be sure that I come outside in a few minutes. Without being followed by your two young assistants."

His face was now an unhealthy greenish colour. "What do you want?"

I smiled. "That's easy. I want to buy the Green Door Hotel."

I couldn't see behind the lens of his glasses but I could see his shoulders relaxing, hear the faint sigh of relief.

So I let him have it in a couple of crisp sentences.

"Kidnapping is a serious crime, Mr Lee. Even when you don't cross state lines. And assault and battery carries a stiff sentence, too. But that doesn't even touch the civil liabilities, Mr Lee. For physical harm suffered and mental anguish, oh, and medicines and fright, that sort of thing, I'm sure I could find a lawyer who'd sue you for around five hundred thousand dollars."

Sweat glistened on his forehead, trickled down his cheeks. He tried to speak, couldn't, tried again.

"I don't know what you're talking about!"

I didn't say a word.

He drew his handkerchief from his pocket, patted his face. "Your . . . accusations are fanciful." He breathed deeply, began to speak more rapidly, "I must insist that you leave my office at once. You are obviously disturbed, overwrought. I have no idea . . ."

"It's in the cellar."

He sat very still, an animal scenting danger.

"The cellar?" The words came unwillingly. He didn't want to ask.

I nodded. "Yes. I signed my name. In blood. You'll never find it. But I can tell the police where it is. And they'll find my fingerprints. And Jimmy's, of course."

He didn't say anything.

"You shouldn't have been so greedy, Mr Lee. It doesn't pay, you know. Jimmy was going to give you the fossils in exchange for the hotel and now, now you are going to sell the hotel to me for seventy-eight thousand dollars . . ."

His face twisted in dismay.

". . . in cash and other considerations. I have the contract here with me."

I handed it to him.

He took it. I moved around to the side of his desk, making sure about that buzzer. When he had read the contract through, he began, "If you will leave it with me . . ."

I shook my head. "No, Mr Lee. You are to call your attorney and we will go now and sign the contract. I have witnesses waiting."

"Where?" His voice was dull.

"Why, Mr Lee. At the Green Door Hotel, of course."

That evening, I opened a bottle of champagne when Dan came. I waited until after dinner, beef stroganoff and rice and a green salad, before I told Dan about my day. Sort of. We were on the couch and his arm was around me. "Dan, I have a hypothetical case I'd like to tell you about."

The nice thing about hypotheticals is that no one has to act on information received.

When I had finished, he was striding up and down the living room, sweeping his hand through his hair.

"My God," he said simply when I was done. He looked at

me, shook his head, then plumped down on the couch beside me.

"Ellen . . ." He cleared his throat. "Ellen, my God! Blackmail. Duress. Extortion. My God."

I said demurely, "But the contract says a sale for seventy-eight thousand dollars and other considerations."

That drove him off the couch again. He strode to my bay window then swung around and came back to look down on me, his legs spread apart, his hands on his hips.

"You need a keeper," he muttered. "You and Jimmy and Miss Chow; my Lord, the streets of San Francisco aren't safe with the likes of you running about."

I was admiring the long lean lines of his face and the way his mouth moved and the breadth of his shoulders and the powerful stand of his legs and . . .

"Ellen!"

"Hmm?"

"You aren't listening!"

I laughed. "No. I was thinking . . ."

"What?"

"Oh, rather scientifically."

He sat down beside me again. "You don't look scientific."

In a moment, a long moment, I said breathlessly, "Heterosis."

"Sounds like a sick fish."

I grinned. "No. As a matter of fact, it's a biological term. It means hybrid vigour."

He didn't say anything.

"You know," I explained, "when you cross independent strains of plants and animals, the first generation usually shows a marked increase in size, strength, vigour . . ."

For just an instant, he looked shocked, then amused. He threw back his head and roared with laughter.

"It means," I said with some dignity, "that we should have magnificent children."

"And a magnificent time producing them," he added happily.